W9-AGM-343

American Short Fiction

PUBLISHED IN COOPERATION WITH
THE TEXAS CENTER FOR WRITERS
Rolando Hinojosa Smith, Director,

AND WITH THE SOUND OF WRITING,
A SHORT STORY MAGAZINE OF THE AIR,
BROADCAST ON NATIONAL PUBLIC RADIO,
Caroline Marshall, Executive Producer

$\mathcal{A}$MERICAN $\mathcal{S}$HORT $\mathcal{F}$ICTION

Volume 2, Number 7, Fall 1992

LAURA FURMAN
Editor

CATHERINE VANHENTENRYCK
SUSAN WILLIAMSON
JOHN ZUERN
Editorial Assistants

JOHN KINGS
Managing Editor

Editorial Advisory Board

ARTURO ARIAS   CYNTHIA MACDONALD
DAVID BRADLEY   JAMES MAGNUSON
ALAN CHEUSE   JAMES A. MICHENER
FRANK CONROY   ELENA PONIATOWSKA
ELIZABETH WARNOCK FERNEA   JUDITH ROSSNER
TONY HILLERMAN   LESLIE MARMON SILKO
FRANCES KIERNAN   TED SOLOTAROFF
JOSEPH E. KRUPPA   WILLIAM WEAVER
OWEN LASTER   WENDY WEIL

Editorial Staff
KATHERINE HESTER   JESSICA REISMAN

UNIVERSITY OF TEXAS PRESS

AMERICAN SHORT FICTION, established in 1991, is published four times a year in Spring (March), Summer (June), Fall (September), and Winter (December) by the University of Texas Press in cooperation with the Texas Center for Writers and "The Sound of Writing," a short story magazine of the air broadcast on National Public Radio. The editor invites submissions of fiction of all lengths from short shorts to novellas. All stories will be selected for publication based on their originality and craftsmanship.

STYLE *The Chicago Manual of Style* is used in matters of form. Manuscripts must be double-spaced throughout.

MANUSCRIPTS AND EDITORIAL CORRESPONDENCE Please send all submissions to: American Short Fiction, Parlin 108, Department of English, University of Texas at Austin, Austin, Texas 78712-1164. Only those manuscripts received between September 1 and May 31 are accepted and considered. Please accompany submissions with a stamped self-addressed envelope sufficient for the return of your manuscript and our correspondence.

SUBSCRIPTIONS (ISSN 1051-4813) · Individuals/$24.00; Institutions/$36.00. Foreign subscribers please add $5.50 to each subscription order. Single Copies: Individuals/$7.95; Institutions/$9.00. Send subscriptions to: American Short Fiction, Journals Division, University of Texas Press, Box 7819, Austin, Texas 78713. All prices are subject to change on September 1 of each year.

CLAIMS POLICY Domestic claims for missing issues must be received within 90 days of the publication date. Non US claims for missing issues must be received within 180 days of the publication date.

Copyright © 1992 by the University of Texas Press, Box 7819, Austin, Texas 78713. All rights reserved. Printed in the United States of America. No part of this journal may be reproduced in any manner whatsoever without permission except in the case of brief quotations embodied in critical articles or reviews. For information write Permissions, University of Texas Press, Box 7819, Austin, Texas 78713.

Excerpt in "Spirit Voices" by Dan Chaon is from the book *Adelaide and the Night Train* by Liz Rosenberg (New York: Harper Collins, 1989).

Design and typography by George Lenox

COVER: *Los Lingos Canyon, Texas,*
photograph by Dan Flores

CONTENTS

THE EDITOR'S NOTES

*R*eading may be the last private act of our lives. We talk openly, and our fellow citizens are polled constantly, about sex, marriage, family troubles, political and religious beliefs. Writers are traditionally asked about their writing habits, as if by knowing what time of day and where a habitual act takes place, we can better understand the text that results. But few people are asked about their reading habits: Where do you like to read and at what time of day or night? Do you do it lying down or sitting up, eating or drinking at the same time? Does it drive you crazy if there's music playing?

Until I began to edit *American Short Fiction,* I had only a dim notion of my friends' reading habits. In the fiction classes I teach, I refer to The Reader, what is going to stop The Reader, what is going to help The Reader. I assumed that The Reader was intelligent, alert, skeptical but willing to be convinced—not unlike a friend. Charlotte Brontë must have had such a sympathetic listener in mind when she had Jane Eyre confide, "Reader, I married him."

Many of my friends read before they fall asleep, and since they lead busy lives, working one or two jobs, tending a house, a family, themselves, they are tired at the end of the day. The time when they read before sleep is an encapsulation of what is supposed to happen when you go on vacation. The daily round of obligations, duties, and appointments is over; however well or badly you've done, it is too late to alter a thing. Reading before sleep puts you in a safe blue harbor where you forget where you are and who you are, for as long as you manage to stay awake and involved. It doesn't seem to matter if you are reading disturbing, moving, tragic stories; those troubles are not yours, though for a moment you believe they are. Some of my friends read—fiction, at least—as a last resort when even sleep fails them. Fiction, particularly short fiction, suits the insomniac who cannot or does not wish to do anything useful but is too anxious to sleep. One friend read two issues of *American Short Fiction* before falling asleep. I wondered how her dreams were peopled—Reynolds Price's feathered man, Susan Fromberg Schaeffer's scientist who suspends his life to watch his cat die—or if she was so filled with characters and events that her sleep was soundless and black.

When I was a child I loved reading before sleep, but I also read on rainy afternoons and when I was supposed to be doing my homework, Nancy Drew and Nero Wolfe contributing at different periods to my delinquency. I read during car rides to the country and later on long bus rides through Manhattan to high school. Novels gave me a place to stay for a long visit, but short stories held me with such intensity I later sometimes confused what I'd read with what I'd experienced. I prefer not to borrow books because I like to read while I am eating and I'm ashamed to return books splattered with spaghetti sauce. A friend of mine used to commute to graduate school, and his books are filled with almost illegibly scrawled notes, the result of writing while reading while driving. At least reading while eating doesn't risk anyone's life. ✑

MANY MOONS

Oh, Mother, the moon is so pretty tonight,
'Twas never so pretty before. . . .

It was his mother's diction that Tyler remembered even more than her vibrant voice. She pronounced each word with care. She had been trained to sing without a trace of her Texas accent.

She sang at the piano in the living room, at the kitchen sink, at church, and at those moments when she wanted to distract him. She was always animated when she sang, posing, acting out the words, holding his hands, and making him give her his full attention.

Her song about the moon was the first she ever sang just for him, to calm him and get him ready for bed, when he was a baby.

————

Tyler was headed home late on the road out to the ranch, and he drove straight into the moon's white brilliance. It was powerful enough to light the entire West Texas desert. He bounced across the cattle guard, parked under the big oak tree out back, and cut off the motor.

The silence was profound. The spell of the movie he had just seen fell away slowly. The old pickup in the driveway, the stack of tires, the board fence next to the barn, the house with the tin roof, the tractor he had driven all day and fled at sunset to forget the heat and the monotony of row after row—everything now looked mysterious and foreign, drenched in white light.

He got out of the car but did not slam the door. Noise would break the spell. Some plants from his mother's garden seemed to smell especially strong: the ligustrum, heavy and cloying, was in bloom; and its odor was mixed with jasmine, faint rose, and dusty weeds.

He lifted his hands to his face and inhaled. Blended with the chemicals that had been used to fix his date's perfume was something else, moist and ripe and female, that made him feel weak.

He stumbled going up the back stairs. His attic room was so filled with moonlight that there was no need to turn on a light. He pulled off his boots and dropped his clothes on the chair. In the mirror on the closet door his dark sunbrowned face and chest and arms were invisible. From the waist down his pale belly and legs seemed to glow. He was like one of those characters in an ancient Greek myth—only half man.

He turned away and sprawled across his bed. It was too warm for even a sheet.

———

In 1943 Tyler was drafted and sent to the West Coast. He washed pots in a Navy hospital and then was transferred to stand guard duty on the docks at Port Hueneme. His quarters were in a temporary barracks with sixty other men. Every four hours twenty of them got up to go on duty, and shortly after they left, the men they had replaced would come in and stir around, getting into their bunks. The thin-walled building was right on the beach, and the Pacific Ocean pounded against a breaker wall just beyond. How could anyone sleep in such a place? He would lie awake waiting for the flashlight in his face, the rough punch on his shoulder.

Tyler lost weight. He had always been skinny, but he was down to a hundred and twenty pounds. One morning he reported to sick bay. The doctor who saw him was a captain. He was old and red faced with a swollen nose, and he was very drunk.

Tyler told him that since he had worked in a Navy kitchen, he could no longer eat the food. His barracks, Tyler said, were full of noisy lunatics getting up and going to bed for guard duty at all hours. He couldn't sleep. "I feel as if I'm going to fall apart," he said. "I think I may have some kind of collapse."

He wasn't sure for a moment that the doctor had heard him. He waited.

The doctor looked as if he were trying to focus on him. "You are a skinny one, aren't you?" he said gruffly. There was another long silence. A corpsman typed forms in the next room. "Well, son, there are two kinds of men in this world. There are those who are fearful and timid and nervous, and then there are those who just make up their minds that they don't want to be that way. All you have to do is make a decision."

Tyler waited. Was that it? The doctor dismissed him with a curt nod.

Tyler left, furious and more anxious than ever.

That night when he couldn't go to sleep he pulled on his pants and went out to the huge stones that had been piled up to break the surf. He sat and watched the moon. Its cold distance and the indifference of the black Pacific were adding to his sense of panic.

He climbed down onto the sand and walked toward the only building on the base that was permanent, a Maritime Training Center that had been taken over by the Navy. The facade was all glass, blacked out for wartime. Because of the moon, it had become a kind of shimmering mirror wall.

As Tyler approached he saw what appeared at first to be a reflection of the moon, but then he decided it was a bearded giant dressed in a silver robe, just inside the build-ing. Was the figure nailed up on a cross? Tyler thought so, but he guessed at the same moment that he must be hallucinating.

The shadow's head lifted and looked directly at Tyler. The eyes were hypnotic, and gradually Tyler began to feel a piercing calm. The apparition faded. The moon had moved up in the sky.

Tyler went back to the barracks, climbed into his bunk, and fell into a deep sleep. In the morning, for the first time in months, he was starving at breakfast time.

———

The war ended and Tyler went to college in New York City. One morning he woke up cramped, unable to stretch, cold, women's shoes pressing into his back. When he tried to sit up, clothes dangled in his face. The darkness was absolute. His head ached, and he was thirsty.

Yes, he remembered dimly. He had been drinking. There had been a party in an apartment on Riverside Drive, and he and some other guys from the dorm had gone. Then they had moved on to another party down the block . . . maybe they had moved again after that. He couldn't think clearly.

He pushed the hanging clothes away and tried to stand. He was in a closet. He didn't remember any closet. His heart began to pound. He had on no clothes at all. Who had undressed him and put him in here?

He found the small metal doorknob, turned it, and pushed open the door. Bright moonlight streamed into the room. There was a couple in bed. Had he ever seen them before? The girl, who was facing him, was quite pretty, her hair in tangles across a rumpled pillow. He held his breath. If they woke up now, how would he explain what he was doing in their bedroom?

His jacket was hanging on the back of a chair and under

it were his shirt and trousers, all neatly arranged. His shorts and undershirt were on the seat. He dressed quickly and picked up his shoes. His socks were tucked inside them.

He tiptoed from the room, down a dark hall, and through a cluttered living room. At the apartment entrance, he paused to put on his shoes before he opened the door. There was another hallway and then a stairwell. He had never seen any of it before. He walked down and let himself out of the building.

Morning was on the way, but the moon still provided most of the light. The street was paved with stones. He walked to the corner to check the street sign. He was on West End Avenue. He didn't know anyone on West End Avenue.

He shivered in the damp spring air and turned up the collar of his jacket, the only one he had, the one his wealthy aunt in Dallas bought for him when he left for college.

The growing light of day made the moon look drained and weary.

Tyler's infant daughter, asleep in her crib in the moonlight, was a frightening presence. She had so much dark, stiff hair that she looked like an Indian's baby.

"White man promise many moons ago . . ." That's the way Indians talked in movies. Victor Mature, or some other mediocre contract player, trying to look sincere or frightening in loincloth and feathers. As a boy, Tyler and his friends at the Saturday double feature had laughed and hooted.

Generations earlier, a Cherokee girl, along with her family and tribe, was driven from her home in Tennessee. Most died on the wagons west, but she survived and a white man in Texas took her. She had a daughter, and that girl married a white man, and the Indian blood was thinned until Tyler's father said he didn't really believe that there had ever been any mixing at all. But the photograph of Tyler's grandmother showed Cherokee cheeks and eyes and hair. Her sepia silk dress looked like a costume forced on some wild creature, trapped for the photographer.

And here in the moonlight, Tyler watched this papoose snuffling in her blankets. He wondered if she would count the passage of her life by the cycles of the moon.

The summer night fell in Vermont, and Tyler was about to go upstairs to bed when he thought he might walk down to the dock. Just past the trees that lined the shore he spotted the moon. It was full, spectacular in its deep red-orange color, a perfect globe hanging a few feet above the mountains. There was still enough light to see the distinctive shape of Cone Mountain, but the lake was dark, pierced by the rippling shaft of reflection that was bright orange, too.

Tyler took an aluminum chair from the beach out to the end of the dock and sat, staring at this moon. After a few moments, he decided that it was too impressive not to share.

He walked back to the house. Light spilled onto the lawn from the windows. He called in through the screen door to his wife, "Come down to the dock, will you?"

"In a minute." She hadn't eaten much supper and now she was making toast. He could smell it.

He strolled back to the lake where an ancient glacier once lingered a few thousand years too long. He and his wife had been married thirty-nine years.

When she came out to the end of the dock he got up and gave her the chair. He said, "You didn't wear your glasses. I wanted you to see the moon's face. It's never been clearer."

"I can see it if I squint. The eyes, the mouth—it looks like a Halloween pumpkin, doesn't it?"

"It has a nose, too," he said. He slapped at the mosquitoes that had discovered them and then he tried to stand quietly. "I feel very Japanese," he said.

"Ah, yes," she said. "Contemplating the moon is a very Japanese thing to do."

They had been at the Vermont house the summer the two astronauts walked on the moon's surface. Tyler said, "I wonder what they think about when they look up and see it—the men who walked on it, I mean."

His wife mumbled something that he didn't hear. He was growing deaf, but he was tired of asking her what she had said.

"My mother used to sing me a song about the moon," he said.

"Yes," his wife said. "You've told me."

CAMPBELL GEESLIN grew up in Brady, Texas, and earned degrees from Columbia College in New York City and The University of Texas at Austin. He has worked as an editor for *The Houston Post, The New York Times,* and *Life.* Mr. Geeslin is the author of a novel *The Bonner Boys* and edited *The Nobel Century,* a picture book.

DEPOT

The figure, the stranger, was rimmed with flamey light, moving slowly and unsteadily yet with a stubborn momentum along the railroad tracks on the embankment behind the old depot. Alice Brandt, sitting in her deceased father's 1967 Lincoln Continental on an August evening in 1979, merely watched. She had no idea what she might do, might she do anything.

I am not interested in facts any longer but in the motives behind facts.

Yes but you must content yourself with facts.

Facts are accessible, motives are not.

There are no motives. There are facts.

She was thirty-eight years old and trained to be a historian, but she'd begun to lose faith in history just as, since her father's death, she was beginning to see that being loved, even very much loved, makes no difference finally, or not much difference. That this was a fact she'd always known because she was an intelligent, thoughtful woman who knew such things without flinching seemed beside the point, it wounded and perplexed nonetheless. And she was ashamed of herself without knowing why. *You must die and I must live. Must I?*

 American Short Fiction, Volume 2, Number 7, Fall 1992
© *1992 Joyce Carol Oates*

How liquidy-warm and airless the summer, and protracted, hazy as a dream without crisis, yet she wanted it
not to end, she wasn't ready. Often she found herself driving past the old railroad depot on lower South Street only
half conscious of what she did but elated by the prospect
of doing it . . . Alice Brandt the doctor's daughter whom
everyone knew as a strong, forthright, unsentimental person, a woman with a career, yet now again, the second or
is it the third time this week, there she is swinging the big
black Lincoln down along South Street where the pave-
ment turns to gravel and the distinction between the town
of Yewville and the surrounding countryside is uncertain.
Here there are properties whose rear lots are meadows
where horses graze. The pine woods presses close. Even
the sky appears more immediate. In late summer, cicadas
sing their high, shrill, maddening notes more fiercely here,
the tall grasses and trees must be teeming with them, but
of that Alice Brandt is not much conscious, she's come to
park her car by the depot just to sit for a few minutes, to
see yes it's still there. Still.

The depot had been built in 1919, shut down in 1974.

A desolate place, yet retaining its dignity, or was it a sort
of mock-dignity, smudged brick, two stories, with a steep
shingled roof now badly rotted, a partly collapsed platform, tilting overhang. Six-foot thistles and burdocks
and young scrub willow crowding close. Discarded beer
bottles and cans, broken glass, graffiti scrawled on the
walls, and strips of cheap plywood nailed over the windows and doors in ugly *X*'s visible a block away. Local
children had ripped down some of the plywood strips and
shattered what remained of the windows; derelicts (they
were not yet called "homeless" people) sometimes slept in
the depot or were to be seen sitting on the platform. The
aged red brick had now an eroded, chalky look as if per-
petually in shadow.

In her car Alice sat, sometimes for as long as half an hour, thinking of nothing in particular, for, here, there was nothing in particular to think. Vividly she could remember the drama of the old passenger trains, the intensity of childhood emotions generated by train trips, the whistles, the hissing of steam, the drive to the depot from the Brandts' house on Cabot Avenue and the excited fear that the train would pull out before they got there, though adults were always in charge of course, responsibly in charge, and not once in all those years of her seemingly endless childhood had the Brandts missed a train. Most of Alice's train trips were with her mother to visit her mother's relatives in Albany but several times she and both her parents had gone to New York City by Pullman and while she'd been in college at Cornell she had sometimes traveled part of the way by train though it was more practical to drive. Now no passenger trains ran on these tracks, and though freight trains continued on a sharply reduced schedule, were they the majestic trains of Alice Brandt's childhood, Baltimore & Ohio, New York Central, Union Pacific, Central Pacific, Chesapeake, Erie, Mohawk Valley, Lackawana Railroad, Santa Fe Railroad, she very much doubted that they were the majestic trains of her childhood rushing across the trestle above the canal, holding up traffic for blocks on State Street, thunderous, deafening, freight car after car after car tearing at her eyes and their nighttime whistles penetrating her dreams. Now, like everyone else, when Alice Brandt traveled any distance she traveled by plane.

———

This August evening, sitting in her car, motor idling (Alice never turned off the ignition when she was parked here; turning off the ignition would be a signal of a kind she wouldn't want to interpret), she found herself watching the railroad embankment and some movement there emerging from a tunnel-like overhang of trees; there was someone walking on the tracks and Alice couldn't at first determine was it a man or a woman, vague as if glimpsed through fibrillating waves of heat.

She was restless, not very happy. Yes of course she was happy. She was a strong-willed, happy woman unaccustomed to feeling sorry for herself or even to thinking much about herself, but tonight she was thinking how pointless to feel ashamed, if that was indeed the way she was feeling, because she was living and others were not living or, if living, not so healthy and easy and forthright in their bodies as she. She'd just come from a visit with a family friend, an elderly former patient of her father's now invalided at home with Parkinson's disease, and though the visit had been cordial enough and even affectionate she'd felt obscurely guilty and eager to leave. She was one of those people subtly offended by problems for which they themselves can provide no cure.

Afterward, thinking over her experience of this night, Alice would realize that had the person on the railroad tracks been a man and not a woman she would never have approached him.

Not out of fear: she was hardly a fearful person. But out of something difficult to define as *tact*.

It was a woman, disheveled, wearing a man's trousers and what appeared to be a man's shirt, a gauzy scarf knotted around her head and another scarf, or shawl, tied around her shoulders. She walked slowly as a sleepwalker, carrying a duffel bag clasped to her chest. Alice watched with worried eyes. The woman was no one she recognized, in her early thirties perhaps, oblivious of Alice a short distance away and showing not much awareness of her surroundings. Alice wondered if she was ill, or drunk, or mentally unbalanced; had she been hurt (her face appeared to be discolored, a bruise under one of her eyes); was she lost . . .? There were few drifters in Yewville in those years and no people without homes in any public, conspicuous sense. Alice, born in 1941, could not remember the Depression years when men on foot had come to the Brandts' house asking for food, or work, or both, but she remembered family stories of those occasions and how always the Brandts gave help to the degree that they could. Her father was known in Yewville for his unfailing kindness with patients unable to pay him; it wasn't charity really, still less prescribed Christian charity, for Dr. Brandt was a stoic and a humanist if he was anything, but his behavior through his life had been suffused with that sort of emotion, that abstract passion: not Christian charity but Christian love which is so much harder. You can't just turn your back on other people and pretend they aren't there.

And that was true. That sober fact, however debated throughout history, however painful to confront, was true.

So Alice, after having watched the woman on the railroad tracks for a few minutes, decided yes she'd better see what was wrong, if anything was wrong. She did not want to meddle and she did not want to frighten and certainly she did not want trouble, but there seemed nothing else to do but switch off the car ignition, get out, make her way, awkward in sandals and a cotton shirtwaist dress, through a patch of spiky weeds to the embankment. It looked as if the woman was headed out into the country and if she followed the tracks she would be crossing the railroad bridge above the canal in less than a mile, there was a pitiless brainless momentum to her walking, as if she'd been walking for a very long time and had forgotten how to stop.

Alice called out, "Hello? Excuse me—" but the woman seemed not to hear, "—Hello? Miss? I don't mean to intrude, but—" Her voice surprised her as it often did in such circumstances, ringing with an authority she did not feel.

But the woman on the tracks, though she must have heard Alice, did not glance in her direction; stiffening, frightened, she began to walk faster and clutched her soiled duffel bag tighter against her chest. Alice boldly climbed the embankment in front of her to cut her off. She was smiling but adamant. "Excuse me but—is something wrong? Do you need a ride? Some help?" The woman's face was bruised and puffy and slick with oily sweat; her carrot-colored hair was greasy and matted like a sheep's; she was younger than Alice had estimated, and she'd clearly been beaten—there was an ugly plum-colored bruise under her left eye and her fleshy mouth was swollen. She crouched as if to protect herself, glaring at Alice, the whites of her eyes the sickly yellow of old ivory, and a smell as of animal panic lifted from her, but she did not speak, her lips twitched but she did not speak as Alice, frightened herself, continued to smile, to smile hard, and to speak placatingly. In her worldly life she was a college professor and even an administrator so she knew how to speak to people who perceived themselves at a disadvantage. "You've been hurt? Have you been hurt? Is someone after you? Do you need help? I'm Alice Brandt—I live nearby—I'm no one official—I'm not with the police—but I'd be very happy to help you if you need anything—a ride, or a meal, or—anything?"

At first the young woman seemed not to hear, her look was both cowering and belligerent, then, after Alice repeated her offer, and carefully repeated it again, she began to relent; though still doubtful and suspicious, glancing around toward the depot, and Alice's parked car, as if she thought someone else might be there, lying in wait. She mumbled what sounded like, "Don't want no police," and when Alice assured her there would be no police, "Not going to no hospital," all the while clutching her soiled duffel bag against her chest.

On their way to Alice's house Alice learned that the young woman's name was "Amalie," or what sounded like "Amalie"; she was headed for Shaheen, a small country town about fifteen miles north of Yewville, though not quite in the direction in which she'd been walking. Quickly Alice offered, "I can drive you there, it's too far to walk," the words tumbling out with a warmth and a generosity she hadn't known she felt but, hearing it, she felt it, and felt good about it, as if empowered.

Except: she was worried about becoming nauseated.

In such close quarters, even with both front windows of her car rolled down, that was her worry: if she should become nauseated, if she should begin to gag. For a sharp acrid odor as of ashes mixed with rotting fruit emanated from the young woman, or from her duffel bag, or both. Alice had never smelled anything quite like it.

She said, almost gaily, "Amalie is a very pretty name—what is your last name?"

————

Alice Brandt realized one day that she'd grown into one of those women, not muscular, nor really fleshy, who appear at ease in their bodies; their handshakes brisk, their heels firm upon the ground. There was a flush to her cheeks, a healthy breathlessness, blood running quickened and warm. And her eyes quick, too, and bright, perhaps a little too bright, darkly shiny, alert. Her hair was dark and springy and her mouth strongly defined, most at ease, or seeming so, in smiling: she was rather shy by nature but to her surprise behaved otherwise, a natural leader as she'd been called as early as elementary school, one of those students upon whom teachers can rely as if, even in childhood, they can be recognized as adults. She disliked the term *handsome* as it was applied to women but knew it was frequently applied to her . . . though, glimpsing herself by accident in mirrors, she saw and was repelled by something faintly simian in the arrangement of her features and the structure of her jaw.

And she was unmarried of course. She had always been unmarried. There was a look to Alice Brandt, a sound to her very voice, that proclaimed unmarriedness: singularity.

Rarely, in Yewville, where she was known as the daughter of the late, much-loved Nelson Brandt, M.D., did Alice speak of her work. She taught courses in American history at a small liberal arts college in Rochester, sixty miles away, she would very likely be the next dean of the faculty there, but that was her life elsewhere, she thought of it as her impersonal life, and she, Alice, lived in Yewville, in the house in which her parents had lived and she had grown up. And she lived not only in that house but in a matrix of people who knew Alice Brandt and had known her and would know her forever; dense as the organic life in a sheltered pond.

In Yewville, she knew what must be done, what was expected of her. She could not turn her back and pretend it wasn't there.

In secret, not in shame but in secret, Alice had had love affairs. Not many, for she wasn't a promiscuous woman, but the affairs had been intense, passionate, hurtful. In her twenties she'd been drawn in fascination to older men, splendidly unattainable older men, married, or temperamentally incapable of returning the fervor of Alice's love, her need. One of the men, with whom she still corresponded, had been her Ph.D. advisor at Cornell. Another was a prominent Rochester journalist who, like Alice, lived in Yewville for family reasons and commuted to work. Yet another, the one Alice had loved most passionately, a Yewville surgeon attached to the same hospital to which Dr. Brandt had been attached, had seemed genuinely in love with Alice and sincere about divorcing his wife to marry her when circumstances allowed (when, for one thing, Alice could bring herself to tell her father: by this time her mother had been dead for twelve years), but finally after several years this man, too, had detached himself from her; apologetic initially; guilty; then defensive; at last rather cold, tactically formal. When Alice in her distress had pressed him to tell her what had gone wrong he'd hesitated, then confessed something so candid and so deeply wounding Alice had never forgotten the words, or the shock accompanying them: "What can I say, Alice?— I'm afraid you've lost all mystery for me."

Hearing those words, those terrible words, Alice had astonished her former lover by laughing: a harsh sibilant sound: and how immediately she'd turned aside, resisting the urge to slap him hard in the face, the bastard, the hypocrite, and how she'd loved him.

These were facts.

Motives?

———

When Alice turned into the graveled driveway of the house on Cabot Avenue the young woman seated beside her regarded it with narrowed eyes. She sat hunched over the duffel bag on her knees and her forehead creased as she stared. The Brandt house, built in 1842, set back from the street in a deep, elm-shaded lot, was a large colonial with a stone facade, a double row of tall narrow windows, dark green shutters that needed repair but, to the casual eye, looked handsome; the house, overall, needed extensive repairs but, to the casual eye, especially at dusk, looked very handsome indeed. Alice saw suddenly her house through a stranger's eyes and stared as Amalie was staring.

Half in admiration, half in resentment, Amalie muttered, "*You* live *here*"—not a question but a questionable statement.

———

If someone had beaten her it was not of him that Amalie spoke in her rambling, aggrieved voice but of her sister up in Shaheen, she was determined to get there, her sister's place up in Shaheen she'd been trying to get to for a long

long time, a damn fucking long time, Amalie confided in Alice Brandt in a voice tremulous with passion, then flat, uninflected, vague. She was trying to get to Shaheen because there were things belonging to her her sister had taken, and she meant to get them back—"Nobody can't do that to me," she said, "—not to *me*," repeatedly, wiping at her nose with the back of her hand or scratching at her head as if it were her own scalp she meant to injure, "—can't do that to *me*, goddamn it, y'know? Yeah?"

Amalie had a fey, puckish quality, a habit of squinting to emphasize her remarks, a grin, or a grimace, slicing her lower face like a knife blade.

Quickly Alice said, "Oh yes. I mean no. *No*."

"None of them," said Amalie in warning, crinkling her tawny-tarnished eyes, "—none of you. But most of all her. That bitch. *Fucking bitch's got no right*." She paused, eating; chewing her food carefully; her head bent like a dog's over her plate.

It was nearly nine o'clock. Because her teeth gave her pain—Alice supposed that was the problem, though Amalie had not complained—Amalie ate slowly; but steadily, and with appetite; it had taken her an hour to finish the several slices of roast beef and the red-skinned potatoes Alice had set down before her, and she had not touched the garden salad at all. The meal was Alice's, too, a meal of substance, but she had not been able to eat much of it. Her heart knocked erratically in her chest, she had difficulty swallowing. And there was the matter of her visitor's smell.

From time to time, to Alice's chagrin, Amalie paused frowning, and, without the slightest self-consciousness, reached into her mouth with her grimy fingers and extracted a piece of beef to examine, which she might then drop on the table before her or replace in her mouth, chew a bit more, and swallow. As she ate she talked; words flowed from her in gushes; it was required of Alice only that she listen, and nod in agreement, or say "Yes" or "No" or "Is that so." When questioned directly, Amalie shrugged, or did not hear.

For a woman several inches shorter than Alice Brandt, Amalie seemed to take up a good deal of space at the kitchen table. She squirmed about in her chair, she glanced down repeatedly to see that the duffel bag, pressed against her leg, was still there, and safe. Her face was puffily round; her nose snubbed, as if it had been broken; she was missing several teeth, giving her a gat-toothed, winking smile. She'd seemed eager to use Alice's bathroom but she hadn't washed thoroughly—only the palms of her hands were really clean, the backs were still dirty and her fingernails were ridged with grime. Her face had a raw, scrubbed look that exacerbated its bruises, nicks, pimples, but there remained caked dust at her hairline and her neck was creased with dirt. She had not taken off the gauzy dimestore scarf knotted around her head, though she'd removed the shawl and stuffed it into the duffel bag. Certainly she hadn't made any effort to wash her body, there was no evidence she'd changed her clothes: a man's gabardine trousers stiff and stained with filth, and ripped at both knees; a long-sleeved shirt crookedly buttoned to the throat, over another shirt; and battered laced-up shoes, heavy looking as if they were made of cast iron.

Alice thought, Why have I done this?

Alice thought, I couldn't just turn my back.

Intimidated at first, in Alice's house, and embarrassed at the start of the meal, Amalie quickly relaxed; became expansive, familiar. It was almost, Alice thought uneasily, as if she knew her—as if Amalie knew Alice Brandt; had recognized her by the depot. Was it possible?—of course it wasn't possible but *was* it possible?

If so, this would explain why the young woman would cast a look at Alice across the table, and say, with that insinuating grimace, "*You* know how it is—a lady like you, Mrs. Brandt?"

Once, to Alice's embarrassment, Amalie said, waving her fork at Alice's plate, "*You* ain't hungry tonight, Mrs. Brandt?—why's that?"

Alice said, smiling, "I'm not 'Mrs. Brandt.' 'Mrs. Brandt' would be my mother. I'm not married."

Amalie, paused in her chewing, beads of perspiration gleaming on her face, said, squinting, "You live all alone here? Yeah?"

"Yes," said Alice, "I live all alone here."

Amalie stared, considering this fact, scratching at her head. Eating had clearly invigorated her; the bruise under her left eye throbbed with a heat and an appetite of its own. It was impossible to judge whether she was naively sincere, or slyly mocking, saying, "Jesus ain't that *nice,* that's real *nice,* you're the *nicest* lady I ever met inviting me back like this, wouldn't hardly anybody be so *nice* except, y'know, the welfare people, but they're shits, or the hospital people," and here she shuddered, as if recalling something upsetting, speaking now of a hospital, or hospitals, in which she'd spent some time, and Alice asked her what sort of hospital was it, and where, but Amalie ignored the question, talking now quickly and agitatedly, leaning toward Alice as if she and Alice were old, intimate friends, "*You* know: you can't let them get their hands on you, like that last time," and Alice, confused, said, "Oh no. I mean yes. Yes—you can't."

Amalie hid her face in her hands suddenly, and said, giggling, "Don't look at me so *hard!*"

Amalie returned then to the subject of her sister, and how she'd wronged Amalie, what a bitch and a liar she was, there seemed, too, to be a baby involved, a baby that had died or had been allowed to die, and speaking of this Amalie's sallow face darkened with blood, her eyes brimmed with tears, and Alice found herself gripping the edge of the table in the sensation of being entrapped in a dream in which she was stuck, paralyzed, mired in mud, for Amalie was saying how long it was she'd been trying to get to Shaheen, a long long time, people always tried to stop her and put their hands on her but this time she meant to do it, to get there—"Nobody better get in my way." She spoke, too, in an excited voice of other places, of "Trinity," "Childwold," and other people, mumbled names that naturally meant nothing to Alice Brandt, though Amalie alluded to them as if they did, and must.

"*You* know that place, Mrs. Brandt," she said; and, with an angry laugh, "*You* know the kinds of things that fucker does, Mrs. Brandt, huh?"

Alice, feeling very uncomfortable, said, as if in commiseration, "I don't know really, Amalie, but—I think you must be right."

Said Amalie, grunting, "Goddamn I *am* right."

When Amalie finished eating she pushed her plate away and asked Alice was there anything to drink, she'd sure like some beer, and Alice, not entirely truthfully, said no there wasn't any beer in the refrigerator, and Amalie shrugged, and grinned, saying, "*You* don't drink beer I guess, Mrs. Brandt?" and Alice flushed as if caught out in a lie, but smiled, and said, "I'll make us some coffee, how's that?" and Amalie nodded yes, yes she'd sure like some coffee, there was a time in her life she'd had all the coffee to drink she wanted: she'd been waitressing up in New Canaan, did Alice know where that was?

Alice said, "I don't think so. No."

It was ten-thirty. The cicadas were singing close outside the windows, that high, shrill, pitiless din that reaches a crisis at about this time in late August, then declines into September with the coming of cooler nights. Listening to them as, with shaky hands, Alice prepared coffee, she thought, bemused, perhaps envious, Ceaseless repetition, every moment the present tense, no memory, and turning back to the stranger slouched at her kitchen table, the stranger who had eaten her food without a word of thanks, Alice cleared her throat, and asked a question she had been hoping to ask for hours, "Amalie, who are you? Where are you from?"

Amalie shrugged, saying, with a just-perceptible sneer, "Oh—nowhere you'd know, Mrs. Brandt."

Alice thought, No history no memory.

She was thinking hard, but no thoughts came to her.

She said, "Well. Can you tell me who hit you?"

Again, with that subtle sneer, "Nobody you'd know, Mrs. Brandt."

Alice said sharply, "I'm not 'Mrs. Brandt.' I've explained—I'm Alice. The woman who was 'Mrs. Brandt' in this house, my mother, has been dead fourteen years."

Amalie, picking between her front teeth with a fingernail, seemed unimpressed with this fact. She said, shrugging, "There's lots been dead longer than *that*."

———

Did she want to sleep in Alice Brandt's house that night, well, she didn't know, maybe she could leave now, just go back to where she was walking, yes but Alice was saying why didn't she take a good warm soaking bath and wash her hair and sleep in a real bed and in the morning Alice could drive her to Shaheen, it wouldn't be any trouble, well maybe she could, well no maybe she could leave now if Alice would drive her back to the depot? to the railroad tracks? she was glancing over her shoulder, squinting and grimacing as if fearful that someone was waiting for her elsewhere in the house, though Alice assured her that she, Alice Brandt, lived alone in the house, had lived alone in this house for the past three years since her father's death, and finally Amalie shrugged and said all right she guessed she could stay now, gripping her duffel bag in her arms again and glancing from side to side jerkily as a tethered horse might, trying to anticipate from which side danger would spring.

Alice said, puzzled, "No one is going to hurt you, Amalie, you must know that by now," and Amalie said with a weak sort of belligerence, "Nobody better put their fucking hands on *me*."

The guest room Alice had prepared for Amalie was at the rear of the house, downstairs. And there was an adjoining bathroom where, briskly, like any solicitous hostess, Alice drew a bath, "—First thing in the morning, after breakfast—I'll drive you—" raising her voice cheerily to be heard over the gushing faucets, "—Shaheen. You need to get a good night's—" aware of her reflection in the bathroom window, faceless, wraithlike yet looming large, backlit against the night.

In the other room Amalie was moving nervously and dispiritedly about, peering at the ceiling, the fussy floral wallpaper, the antique brass bed with the dazzling white hand-knitted afghan spread. Scratching distractedly at her head, her underarms, even her crotch, she said, "Uh— there's nobody else lives here," not as a question but, again, as a questionable statement, and Alice said at once, "I've told you, Amalie. I live alone here." Adding, as if this fact were required, "My bedroom is upstairs."

Amalie muttered what sounded like, "Huh!"

Alice had dutifully laid out thick towels for her guest in the bathroom; she'd unwrapped a fresh bar of fragrant soap; located a tube of shampoo in the medicine cabinet. And would the poor woman need a comb, a hairbrush?— her hair was so densely matted, it must be dreadfully snarled. *But you need not help her with it, that isn't required.* Next, Alice hurried to fetch freshly laundered clothes— clothes of her own: a nightgown, a cotton blouse, a pair of navy blue linen slacks. Casually she said, "Take these or leave them, Amalie, whatever you like. I'll see you in the morning." Amalie, who had still not taken off her absurd dime-store scarf, nor unbuttoned even the topmost button of her shirt, seemed not to have heard. She was staring toward the bathroom with an expression of profound worry—did the sound of the gushing faucets confuse her?—the smell of the bath gel Alice had poured into the tub?

"Amalie? Good night."

The sickly-tarnished eyes caught at Alice's, and in that instant Alice saw terror in them.

There came the nearly inaudible mutter, "Yeah—g'night."

———

Alice was dreaming of an incident her father had spoken of not to her directly but in her hearing for how otherwise did she know about it though perhaps she hadn't known of it from him but by way of others and in the dream there it floated, the dead and partly decayed infant discovered in the water tank of a public toilet in Yewville, one of the women's lavatories in the park near the bus station, years ago and Alice had been in seventh grade and she'd never acknowledged that she knew for certainly she would never have spoken of such a horror to her parents especially such a horror with female and physical and sexual implications, and there it was, poor thing, poor creature, they'd lifted the porcelain back of the water tank and discovered it and had the mother ever been found? the mother, the murderess? the desperate and probably unwed young woman?—had anyone ever been named?

Alice woke to a sound somewhere in the house, thinking, The duffel bag, the smell. Yes.

———

She had not locked her bedroom door. She told herself there was no need.

Hearing the sound, an unmistakable tinkle of breaking glass, Alice thought, There it is. A veritable swoon of excitement and dread washed over her and for a long moment she was too weak to move.

Then, hurriedly, with trembling hands, she put on a bathrobe, and went downstairs barefoot, switched on the hall light to see the young woman—for an instant she'd forgotten her name: Amalie—crouching in front of the living-room doorway. She was fully clothed, the scarf was still tied around her head, she was swaying, clearly drunk. Her sallow pug face was both fearful and insolent: she had apparently opened the door of an antique breakfront cabinet in the hall, and one of Alice's mother's German porcelain figurines had fallen to the floor and broken. Alice said faintly, "What are you doing?"

Alice could smell whiskey from ten feet away. The woman must have discovered the small cache of liquor in a cupboard in the kitchen.

Amalie said loudly, "Don't you touch me."

Alice said, shocked, hurt, "You've been—drinking? What have you done?"

Amalie stood her ground, crouching like a boxer. Her bloodshot eyes gleamed. "Don't you put your hands on me, bitch! None of you!"

Alice said, protesting, "You've misunderstood—"

Then to Alice's horror Amalie began dancing about, taunting, defiant, with a childlike nervy bravado, raising her drunken voice as if in parody of Alice's, though in fact Alice Brandt's voice was a low contralto, "*Nice lady! Nice rich lady! Nice rich fucking lady! Monkey-ugly lady! Monkeybitch!*" She was dipping and swaying; flailing her arms about clownishly. The sound of her own high-pitched voice seemed to excite her. "*I* can be nice like you, gimme your fucking money fucking lady, monkey-face lady, *I* can be *nice* as you are"—hitting the glass door of the cabinet with the back of a hand and breaking it, wincing, laughing, as another object, a small vase, toppled to the floor and shattered.

Alice, standing on the stairs, pressed her hands against her ears. She cried, "Stop—*stop!*"

Amalie laughed rowdily, daring to advance to Alice, to stoop and peer up into her face. "Hey! Monkey-ugly! Gimme your money, huh? C'mon—"

It seemed to Alice, transfixed with horror, that Amalie rushed at her, and in the confusion of the moment Alice struck out, as one might defend oneself against an assault by some flying feathered wing-beating creature in the dark, she heard her voice rising, near-hysterical, "—Get *out!* Get *away!* You don't know me! You're trash and your words are trash and—" Scarcely knowing what she did Alice swung her arm wide to bring the palm of her right hand hard and flat against the other's jeering face, an open-handed blow that sent Amalie staggering backward.

Alice cried, "You don't know me! You have no right! Take your filthy things and get out of my house! *You don't know me!*"

Through a vertiginous red haze she saw the woman slouched against the wall, wiping at her bleeding mouth, staring at her fingers, and at Alice, with incredulous eyes.

———

It wasn't until dawn that Alice had recovered sufficiently to enter the guest room, steeling herself for what she might find—the bedclothes soiled and dragged onto the floor, pillows tossed about, the afghan Alice's mother had knitted in her final illness stained as if that terrible woman had wiped her shoes on it. The bureau drawers had been yanked open and their contents, mainly linens, were disarranged with a pointless malevolence.

The woman had apparently lain on the bed, drinking. In her filthy clothes, in those shoes. Overturned on the carpet was a bottle of whiskey; the air reeked of both whiskey and the woman's sickly sweet odor.

Alice, gagging, pushed the windows as high as she could manage. It was cooler outside now, but the air lay humid and heavy against the house, stale as an exhaled breath.

The tub was still full in the bathroom. The water was tepid, its surface stippled with tiny bubbles; Amalie had not taken a bath, though one of the bath towels was soaking wet and water had been slopped onto the tile floor. Alice steeled herself as she plunged her hand into the water, however, as if she were thrusting it into a poisonous substance.

She listened with satisfaction as the water drained out.

Then she discovered that the toilet was unflushed, so quickly she flushed it, almost gagging again, and there was the toilet tank and what was there about the tank?—biting her lower lip Alice watched as with shaking hands she reached out to lift the tank top, to see what was inside, but of course there was nothing inside except the plumbing fixtures, a grimy floating ball and rusted attachments and some five inches of dank water. What had she expected to find?

Since there was hardly any question of returning to bed Alice began the day early, went upstairs to her own bathroom and hurriedly showered and dressed and returned to the guest room to clean it, removing bedclothes from the bed, and the mattress cover as well, and folding the afghan carefully in preparation for taking it to the dry cleaner's. She gathered up all the towels in the bathroom, several embroidered hand towels and the washcloths, everything, though that woman had not touched most of them, and this time she did not so much as glance at the toilet tank. She did two loads of laundry; she hauled the vacuum cleaner into the guest room to vacuum, and it was while vacuuming the carpet that she felt a curious tingling sensation on her scalp and almost simultaneously a similar sensation on her left forearm, and she squinted seeing the tiny thing, the louse, scurry to lose itself in the fair brown hairs on her arm.

———

In the spring of 1980, to the surprise of everyone who knew her, Alice Brandt sold the house on Cabot Avenue, along with most of its furnishings, and moved to an apartment in Rochester; then, the following spring, she moved again, this time more permanently, to Saratoga Springs where she'd accepted a position at Skidmore College.

In time, she would marry.

Of course Alice returned to Yewville occasionally, for weddings, illnesses, funerals; visits to the cemetery; visits with her past. It was "hers," that past, yet it had become impersonal; not indistinct but impersonal; as if it were an account in one or another of the historical annals in which she did her research. Always in Yewville Alice drove down lower South Street to see the old railroad depot, still standing, years later, in its weedy, littered lot; anxious to know whether the building had been demolished at last.

But it remains. Year following year. Weather-worn, desolate, disfigured by graffiti and those plywood *X*'s over the windows, yet with its old dignity, the aged red brick with that smudged look, even in full daylight, like a dream only obliquely recalled, even in full daylight. ᪅

JOYCE CAROL OATES is the author of more than twenty novels and many volumes of short stories, poems, and essays as well as plays. Her story "Where *Is* Here?" appeared in *American Short Fiction* Number 1, Spring 1991. She lives in Princeton, New Jersey, where she is the Roger S. Berlind Distinguished Lecturer in Creative Writing at Princeton University. Her latest book is *Black Water,* a novel.

STANDARDS

I ZAHA CHATS WITH A SERIAL KILLER

$\mathcal{R}$ight from the beginning, I've had high standards. My dad named me Babe Didrikson Zaharias Dunn just so he could call me Babe; but I didn't want to be Babe, no baby wants to be Babe. I wanted to be Zaharias, because it sounded like Ozzie and Harriet mushed together. Now I think anyone who wants to be named after a sitcom should be taken out and shot, as a personal favor, when very young.

I'm thirty-nine now, in case I haven't mentioned it yet. That next birthday is going to be a killer.

But I still have high standards—about the work I do, for example. It's important to do something truly fulfilling. Something that makes you a whole person. You don't want to count the hours at work as lost time, time when you pretend to be someone less than you are. You're a thinking, responsible, intelligent, creative being. Me, I type for a living.

I go downtown, I go up in the elevator, I sit down. I flick a switch on the side of my computer, and I forget what happens next. Eight and a half hours later I ride the elevator down.

American Short Fiction, Volume 2, Number 7, Fall 1992
© *1992 Ken Chowder*

On the other hand, there's lunch. I eat.

I'm not fat. Just overweight. I'm short; everyone in my family is short, except my sister Trudy, who's an exception. We're short and square and look like the cartoonist hasn't bothered to draw in all the features, except Tru, who's an exception.

I'm short, but I have high standards. I have a spacious studio apartment on Russian Hill, so most of my things are in storage. It's lovely, Russian Hill: the tourists snapping shots at crooked, hydrangeaed Lombard, the cable cars gently cling-clanging up Hyde, and me out there with an AK-47 firing off my nightly rounds at the cable cars gently cling-clanging in the middle of the fucking night.

I love this city, there's no place like San Francisco. Once thieves broke into my last boyfriend's car outside Le Petit Cafe on Larkin and took his tennis racket and his pasta machine. It still makes me shudder to think of those things in the wrong hands.

That last boyfriend was named Gerund. We broke up four years ago. But I have high standards in regard to boyfriends. Gerund had long hair and was short and fat; it'll be hard to find someone as good as Gerund. I don't think I'll be replacing him soon.

So it struck me as extremely peculiar behavior, this thing I did in the office the other day. I couldn't even explain it to myself.

You wonder how people explain themselves. Let's say you could get down to basics with a serial killer over coffee. "So, you strangle people," you'd say. Your serial killer would nod; you'd ask, "Why, incidentally, would you *want* to strangle people?" And he'd say, "Well, Zaha, it just seems like a great idea at the time."

Which is probably the reason why, the other day, I asked this guy at work if he wanted to go out with me.

I work for the biggest legal firm in the city: Taxshelter, Loophole & Ambulancechaser. We have hundreds of lawyers. I'm not going to break out our lawyer jokes, but it's true: cockroaches and stool samples are far better company than lawyers. But recently a very interesting man started work in Word Processing. Possibly the most interesting thing about him was that he was a man. But maybe not. He's named David. David isn't as short and fat as Gerund, but he does have a wandering eye and the habit of smacking his lips as he types, as if chomping on a nice tort. David has huge glasses and all the facial structure of Play-Dough—cute, in other words.

You know how it goes. We started hanging out together at the coffee maker. We started talking about TV, because TV is the great common denominator, everybody watches TV. Neither of us watches TV. It was amazing. David reads books instead. I felt very sorry for him, though I also read books. And then it turned out we'd read *the same book* once. It was amazing, really.

So I asked him—as if it were the most natural thing in the world—if he'd like to go out and do something.

We were just getting off work. David exited his software and turned to me. "You mean," he said, "together?"

"I don't know," I said. "Well, actually, yes. Maybe. If you wanted to. But who knows?" I said.

"OK," David said. "When did you want to go out?"

We are a dark and mysterious species. Our race has produced fast-food franchises, serial and mass murderers, and daytime TV—that is to say, we don't always act sensibly. I, to take one perfectly random example, suffer from Groucho Marx Syndrome.

So I took a good look at this guy, this David. It was like he *wanted* to go out with me. Something was wrong. There were lots of women with sparkling, fawn-colored hair in Word Processing, and none of *them* seemed to be asking David for a date. Why not? He was fairly tall, David—too tall for me—the guy was almost criminally tall.

That wandering eye was really a sad badge. And what did I want to do, go out with someone who *types* for a living? We'd have a lot to say over dinner; we could discuss the way the em key felt under our right index fingers that day. And it didn't seem likely that we'd both read the same book *again* sometime. What did seem likely, though, was that he was a serial murderer, probably a strangler, whose modus operandi was to infiltrate word-processing pools at law firms, then strangle his coworkers, one by one.

"You mean, together?" I said to him.

"What did you have in mind?" he said.

Warning. Warning. Danger. Unsafe. Life-threatening. Steer clear, watch out, go back; I was doing a little Doppler effect in my head, like a siren screaming along a street.

"I don't know," I said. "Maybe you could come to my house. For dinner." Not that I can cook. Actually, I *can* cook, I just won't. But my house was the only safe place in the universe. Never mind that the floor of my place is littered with books. It would make good conversation. I could build a little igloo of books and get inside, and David could make his own little igloo and get inside *it,* and we could just read a while. There were tons of things we could do, David and I, so long as we didn't have to look at each other or, of course, speak.

"OK," he said. "When?"

I could invite my sister too, for protection. Maybe he'd decide to kill her first; as his hands closed around her beautiful white neck, I could run screaming to the police, safe as houses.

"Umm, Saturday," I said. "Any Saturday."

"How about this Saturday?"

"How about three weeks from this Saturday," I said.

He said the dumbest thing then. "OK," he said. The guy was *smi*ling, even. What had I done?

II ZAHA ENTERTAINS IN PATAGONIA

Zaha woke up in an indeterminate section of the late morning and thought, David's coming tonight: lunacy. He was coming for dinner; he'd probably be expecting her to give him *food*. After that he'd probably be thinking about strangling her with her nylons. Now where the hell were her nylons again? Never mind; he'd find them.

Trudy showed up in the afternoon, obnoxiously on time, as usual. Tru wore black Levi's, which looked, by some trick, fantastic, and an Academy of Sciences T-shirt with repeated images of black fish in white squares. She looked stunning, sunny, warm, and cool, all of which annoyed Zaha for the millionth time. But you try it some-time: grow up with a little sister who does a close approxi-mation of perfection and doesn't even notice—while you are, at your absolute best, a human being. Try living up to impossible standards, just once; your own standards get lower and lower.

Soon Tru was picking up and putting away a few of Zaha's books. But what was so wrong with the *floor,* anyway? "Amazing collection of travel books," Tru said. "You must know everything about Africa."

"Africa was a phase," Zaha admitted. "Then Patagonia was a phase. Until they came out with those outdoor jacket-things that feel like hot pads."

Tru straightened up, holding a batch of Patagonias. "So who's this guy coming over tonight?"

"His name is David or something. I don't actually know the guy. He types." Zaha picked up a book, inspected its back cover closely, and dropped it. "Well, anyway," she said. "He's a very good typist, actually. Very fast, at least."

"What does he look like?"

She squinted out the window; it was so pathetically *bright* out there. "Oh, he looks kind of—kind of the way you'd picture a ghost, if there was such thing as an *actual* ghost. Not a movie ghost. Like a living dead person. He's got a wandering eye."

"Like Sartre," Tru said—soothingly, maybe.

"No, not like Sartre. I don't even *like* this guy. I'm not about to give him the Nobel Prize."

Tru looked a little shocked. She had her own standards, after all. "Why don't you like him?"

Zaha shrugged. "He's got a face like an ironing board. Plus the guy's murdered women in four states."

"Zaha?"

"Hey, what are you doing with those books, *reading* them? Time's a wastin', girl. You got yourself some dinner to cook yet."

———

David showed up in jeans and a flannel shirt, and she thought: Guess he doesn't think this is any too important. Of course he's right. We just give him his damn dinner and get him out of here before he finds the nylons.

God, those glasses are *thick*. The world must be a complete blur to him. No wonder he's here.

He handed her the flowers, in stapled white paper. "Roses," she said. "How nice. Red roses. Unusual color for roses, red." Then she saw how Tru was looking at her. She'd have to stop this, is what she'd have to do. She'd really have to stop. "Never liked the smell of roses much," she said. "Too kind of—floral, you know?"

David's shoulders did a little crane dance. "I never minded it."

"No. Of course you didn't. Well, come on in."

He looked around the place. "Amazing," he said. "I've never heard of using rubber plucked chickens as—as a motif."

"You know, it just happens. You get one plucked chicken, then all your friends think Plucked Chicken every Christmas." He walked around, examining chickens.

"So," she said. "I forgot to give you the Proper Ritual Chant to offer the Parking God. You probably had a ton of trouble."

"I took Muni. I don't have a car."

"Don't have a car!" Zaha said. "My lands! What country do you think this is, Romania? Anyway. This is my sister, Trudy."

They shook hands. "Trudy," David said, a little reverently.

"I've heard good things about you," Tru said.

"Yeah?" David said. His eyebrows folded, moved closer together. "What things?"

"Yes, Trudy," Zaha said. "What things?"

"Unh. Zaha says you're a—really good typist. And she has very high standards."

David made a mystified smile. "We do that for a living," he said. "After a while you stop being good at it."

Trudy looked confused: she was too good at things, she'd never know what it was like to do nothing well. Zaha herself, for example, wasn't good at sleeping; she was a bad doodler; she suspected she didn't even breathe correctly. "David's right," she said. "It's not you doing the typing. It just gets done." She glanced over at David; he wasn't looking quite at her. "Your fingers are good at it," she said, "but you're not personally involved. It's like being a Nazi peon at Auschwitz. You let your fingers do the gassing."

"It can't be that bad, can it?" Trudy said.

"At Huckster, Shyster & Flyright? No, it's not that bad. Many die. Their cries go unheard in the night. But the word-processing pool does its noble work in the gloaming," Zaha said. "Let's take a seat, OK? I'll get a drink."

Zaha and Tru moved toward the chair and couch, stepping over a few books. David just stood there. "A seat. As in, we sit *down*," she said, pointing at the couch. "Down, boy. So what do you want to drink?" she asked. "Red wine is the correct answer."

"That sounds good."

"Exactly what do you type, anyway?" Tru said. "I never asked."

"Oh, you know," Zaha said. "Pleadings. Briefs. Contracts. Declarations of war. Suicide notes."

"Briefs are the longest," David said. "Paradoxically."

There was a brief silence. "I'll get the wine," Tru said.

"No, I'll get it."

"No. I'll get it," Tru said.

"No," Zaha said.

"I'll get it," Tru said, and pushed Zaha back into the plastic chair. Zaha moved the chair a further foot away from the couch where David was. It was an uncomfortably small room, actually; he seemed to be almost breathing in her face. "In the way of very small talk," she said, with some difficulty. "What do you do at home?"

"Not even one thing," David said. He smiled about it. "It's quite amazing, really. What about you?"

"The very same," she said. She was so short that her feet did not quite reach the floor; she could swing her legs, kicking, like a hyper child waiting for the end of arithmetic class. So she did that, and David sat and closely watched her legs kicking; he was almost staring, as if he were fascinated, or else horrified; or maybe just poised on the edge of sleep, and so unable to move.

———

Zaha tugged the meat off the bone with her fork. It came easily, because Tru had done the cooking. She'd roasted the chicken on a bed of carrots, baby artichokes, and fennel. Hey, there were even pine nuts in here. What did Tru do, *travel* with pine nuts? She probably kept a supply of radicchio in her vest pocket.

David was tucking in: he speared himself a drumstick, then a thigh, then a wing, and then the back. He gave each piece a look of high reverence as he dangled it, apparently mesmerized by the parade of chicken parts. "Trudy," he kept saying, "this is *so* good."

"There's more stuff in the pot," Tru said happily. This is how women are supposed to be, Zaha thought: make the food, then live off the compliments.

"I'll go get it," Tru said to David. She pushed away from the little table. David suddenly looked up from his laden plate to give something his full if astigmatic attention; Zaha turned to see what marvel could be redirecting his stare. At first there seemed to be nothing to look at. Then she saw it: it was Trudy. Tru, in jeans. Of course. Exactly how many times does something have to happen before you expect it, girl? Life imitates life, is all.

"I see," she said, "that you are no mere typer, David. You have high standards. You're a secret connoisseur."

It was even possible that his face was reddening. "Well," David said. "This is really good chicken."

She scowled at the chicken—dead, cooked. Then she held out her left wrist. "My lands!" Zaha said. "How wonderful! You still here, after all this time! And the hour so late!"

———

So he was going, finally. "You want those roses back now?" she asked. "We're great recyclers in this casa."

"I'll bring irises next time," he said.

"I'm sure," Zaha said.

Trudy held her hand out a long way in front of her for a shake. "Thanks for cooking," David said. He held onto Tru's hand for a second. Drop that thing, Zaha thought. "I was wondering," David said slowly, "if I—if you would give me your phone number."

"Oh," Tru said. The smile dropped off her face like a

heavy rain running down a steeply slanted roof. "Oh. I don't think—"

"I'll give you her number," Zaha said.

"OK," he said. And then he did a thing Zaha hadn't expected: he leaned all the way down to Zaha's face. He moved his lips on her cheek. It was a kiss, is what it was called. She felt it; she knew what it was. "Thanks," he said. "For the evening."

"David," she said. "Go and—just go take Muni or something, David." He stood in the doorway a second longer, and she was sure he was going to apologize for something. She didn't want to hear it. "No. You didn't have a hat," she said.

III   ZAHA'S LIFE IS BEAUTIFUL

"Life is very beautiful," Zaha said. "This is perfect." She gazed down from the deck at the edge of the Bay, where a little gasoline floating under sun made a shining spectrum. The gas slick looked like a colorful little man gaily waving the stumps of arms and legs. "Everything is in its place," Zaha said. "Everything has a deep meaning, and a nice slow pace, and of course there's lots of flowers, and everybody's wearing black, and they slowly lower the thing down and start tossing the dirt on top."

She was drinking a martini, despite the cold, which she had ordered because she suddenly got to thinking about fifties movies. The chilled glasses. The one-eyed olive. The deep and steadfast hangover. Ray Milland, for instance.

David was having a beer, a draft. He took a sip and got himself a nice little froth mustache. She had to restrain herself from saying, Two hands please, David. She was doing that, though. She was restraining herself.

"It's too bad," David said. "You wait around and

wait around for a good funeral. And then, just before you get to have one, somebody always dies, and it ruins everything."

He turned the good eye in her direction. His glasses made looking at him like gazing through the walls of a fishbowl: his eyeballs seemed to swell, and swim away, as if someone had just thrown food up on the surface.

"Are you sure they know we're out here?" she said. They were out on the deck at the Mission Rock Cafe; this was November, and they were the only ones, strangely enough. Zaha wore her standard woolen blanket, a chic little thing in black and blue, and David an electric blue parka and Cubs cap. "I get Burger Anxiety, at times," Zaha said. "It's a little personality disorder of mine."

"If a Wimpy one," he said.

"David. No jokes," she said. "We no kid about burger. There is a time for seriousness." She looked at her watch. "My lands! Where *is* that food?"

"I told them we were outside," he said. "They'll be right out with our freshly frozen fries." Zaha held up one finger in warning. "That was a fry joke," he said. "A small one. Not a burger joke."

"Forgiven," she said, and she felt this queer little tug from somewhere, God knows where—this little impulse. She fought it off: no smile. For Christ's sake, no smile. But why not?

Just exactly then, of course, she found out why not. "So how's your sister?" David said. "Trudy."

"Yes," she said. "Trudy. You didn't necessarily *have* to drag me here to ask about Trudy. This is how you do it, David. You call up, you say: *Hello, this is David, is this Trudy?* She gets on, you say: *Hi, Trudy, this is David. How are you?*" Zaha yanked her blanket; her neck was fucking freezing. "You want me to take you through it again, step by step?" she said.

"Jeeze," he said. "Touchy." The guy was *smiling* here; somewhere in the universe someone had just told a joke, obviously. "I've got an idea," he said. "*Don't* tell me how your sister is. Tell me—tell what you're reading these days."

"Reading?" she said. "*Reading?*" She was going to eat her burger and drive home. David could take the *bus* home, for example. If buses even ran out to Mission Rock.

She finished the martini. It was good, once you got the hang of it. She was going to start drinking these babies. Ho's Chinese restaurant down on Green, for example. It opened early. She could drink these instead of *lattes.* There was no end to the things she could accomplish; her standards would just go up and up.

"To be frank. To be actually frank," she said, "Trudy's not interested in you. But not to worry, David. Look! Right across that street is the Esprit outlet. Lots of women, many almost as good-looking as Trudy. They've got their manes of fawn-colored hair and their shopping carts rolling and they're looking to *buy.*"

David reached over and fumbled under her blanket until he found her hand, tightly bunched in a fist. He grabbed it, and the waitress came out the swinging door with her platter on her palm, near her fawn-colored hair. "Cheeseburger rare, with fries?" she asked.

David and Zaha looked at each other. "Here," Zaha said.

"And . . .," the waitress said. "Cheeseburger rare. With fries."

"Here," David said, but he didn't drop hold of Zaha's hand. She felt a thumb moving slowly across her knuckles, her white knuckles. The thumb went over and over her lumpy knuckles, going extremely slowly, touching the skin kind of lightly, kind of gently; it kept doing that until the waitress left.

"Don't be a jerk," Zaha said then. She shook off the hand and went for the burger. "I mean, where's the *ketch*up?" she said.

"I'll get some," David said. When he came back with the ketchup, he took his Cubs cap off in what looked like respect for the burger, and took an immense and untroubled bite. Zaha took one of her own; but it was all wrong. She put down the burger. This is what it had come to: she had to put a burger aside.

"Excuse me," she said. "Excuse my fabulous impoliteness. But can we mention that little gambit of before? The hand-holding?"

David, chewing, inserted the slice of Bermuda onion into the text of his burger. "Sure," he said.

"Let's not," she said. "OK? Let's just not do any of that."

"Why not?" he said, and it seemed like the onion was talking.

"OK, let's say we have a relationship. This is how it goes. It's fantastic. You take out the garbage, you know the names of all the dim sum things, men are wonderful. I go out to the Walgreen's in the rain to get Sucrets when you have a cold coming on, women are so sweet. We eat Chinese food twice a week.

"And then one day I say, *Honey, when are we getting together on Saturday?* And you say, *Zaha, I don't want you to assume things,* and I say, *I wasn't assuming, honey,* and you say, *Yes, you were, you were assuming.* And I say, *Well, maybe I was, honey, but we've seen each other every Saturday for nineteen years,* and you say, *Yes, but, well, I'm feeling kind of a little ambivalent right now.* And it's over. Or else one day you say, *Where's my baseball mitt? I left it right here,* and I say I don't know where your baseball mitt is, but maybe I saw it once twelve years ago under your high-school letter sweater in the top shelf in your closet under the stack of *Consumer Report*s behind the barbells on the way to Gramma's house. And you come back and say, *It was there, but I didn't put it there.* So I say, *Well, maybe I put it there, honey,* though I know damn well I didn't; but you're still mad because I *moved* your baseball mitt, and that night we fight over something else, like whether we *had* the Pad Thai last time we came to this restaurant, and when we get home you shout out from the bathroom asking where your *toothbrush* is, and I say it's in the *toothbrush holder,* where it always is, hon, which of course makes you furious because you don't like my *tone.*

"At best, we have a long protracted painful breakup. At worst, we stay together, make each other miserable, and have a kid or two who are even *better* at making us miserable. So let's not," she said, "Let's skip to the end and say, Sure was great for a while there."

She swished a french fry in a big pool of ketchup. She looked at it a second, thought, *Let it bleed,* then bit it in half.

"Would you really?" David said.

"Really what?"

"Would you really go out to Walgreen's in the rain to buy me Sucrets?"

"No," she said. "Not if it was really raining."

"Well," David said. "We've been having a drought for years. It probably won't rain." And here came his hand again; it came over and grabbed hers.

"Do you mind?" she said. "You're finished, but I'm still in mid-burger. I've got miles to go here." She had to put the burger down one more time. "David. I'm not even close to good enough for you. Go find someone really beautiful to make miserable."

"You know what I think? I think you're really beautiful."

"Hey, you know what I think? I think you're lying."

"Well," David said. "You're beautiful enough."

"Get out of my face with that," Zaha said. She drowned the second half of the fry in ketchup; but she didn't have the heart to eat that fry. She shoved her plate away. No standards, that was her problem: no way to judge—David, fries, anything.

"Hey, you finished with those?" David said.

"Go ahead," Zaha said. And she watched, with a despair that was as petty, familiar, and ridiculous as her face in the mirror, as David put away the rest of her fries.

KEN CHOWDER is the author of three novels. He has twice received fellowships from the National Endowment for the Arts and The Ingram Merrill Foundation, as well as the Ludwig Vogelstein Foundation, the Mary Roberts Rinehart Foundation, and the Oregon Arts Commission. His first book *Blackbird Days* won the Harper-Saxton Prize; his short fiction has been selected for an O. Henry Award, a Pushcart Prize, two PEN Syndicated Fiction awards, and a Nelson Algren award. Mr. Chowder was born in Manhattan and raised in New England.

LYNNE SHARON SCHWARTZ

FRANCESCA

thought I knew what my life was. Through most of it I have been sober and single-minded, for the last twenty-odd years studying the curious eruptions of wayward cells, cancer cells. Most of them cause turbulence and ruin, while a few, especially in older bodies, nestle harmlessly in a corner where they can be virtually ignored, though we forget them at our peril. But then something happened. It seems my passage through the world has been generating trails I could never have imagined, and which might be better ignored as well. After all, so much of human history, private history, goes unacknowledged. Yet I find myself unwilling to let this particle rest. It refuses to, in any case. It has reappeared through a turn of fate, and in a troubling, even terrifying form.

I should note, by way of preface, that I have never been a man who had difficulties with women, or who had hurting ways. Now two women are hurt on my account and they will never know why.

Twenty-four years ago, I spent a semester of my senior year of college in Rome, on one of those programs abroad which have become so common. At the time, it was, if not a rarity, at least more of a special privilege than it is today. And so the dozen of us who were chosen set foot in Italy with a giddiness, an almost unreal elation, sharpened and sustained by our knowing—the men, that is—we might well be drafted and sent to Vietnam soon after graduation. Now or never: we must cram all our youth into those five months. And what better place? Our group made some side trips, to Florence, Siena, Ravenna, a few other cities. But mostly we stayed in Rome, which even without any threat of imminent danger, provides giddiness and elation enough. With all that, I have to say I was on the stodgy side, for a young man in those unstodgy years. Not by choice but through shyness and inhibition.

The program was in art history. I was doing a double major—art history and biochemistry. I had trouble making up my mind, though I was leaning toward biochemistry. It was more practical, and I thought my bent for the meticulous and measurable would serve me better there. Still, I kept up the art history major, partly because I wanted the trip. I wanted something to shake me out of my stodginess—I knew it would take shaking from outside. And since my family was poor and I spent my summers working, there was little chance I would get abroad any other way.

An Italian professor of art history at the University of Rome was attached to our group. He had a long, difficult name we had trouble pronouncing; it sounded to me more Greek or Romanian than Italian. He would walk around the city with us, expounding on its architecture, its churches, its history, as well as amble through the museums, murmuring with nonchalant erudition about the paintings, and finally, he conducted a weekly seminar which convened in his large, ornately cluttered apartment in a small street just off the Piazza Navona, where, he explained, gladiatorial contests, chariot races, and all sorts of rowdy festivities were held in ancient days.

This Roman professor, tall, stout, and rather imposing,

with thick strong features, an unruly black mustache, thinning hair, and a genial bemused manner—as if he found us lovable, benign aliens—must have been forty or so, though we naturally saw him as advanced in age. He had an American wife eight or ten years younger than himself, a rangy, firm-boned woman with hair the color of honey and an imperturbably ironic manner, and on seminar nights she would serve us elaborate, rum-drenched pastries with wonderfully muddy coffee in thimblelike cups—translucent white with a rim of gold at the top—and later, dense, sweet, tart anisette liqueur. She had two young daughters, fair-haired like herself, maybe three and five, who would cavort among us babbling in incomprehensible Italian, so that very soon we realized the seminars would not be excessively scholarly or purposeful: we should regard them instead as a way to get an inside look at a real Roman family. Though as one of the girls in our group pointed out, it was hardly a typical Roman family since the wife and mother was American, like us.

She—Janet was the wife's name—did not seem American. So far as I could tell, her clothes, her mannerisms, and gestures were all Roman: decisive, dramatic, mellow. She appeared to have taken on, effortlessly, the coloration of her chosen environment, and when she spoke Italian to the children, which at first we understood only in bits and pieces, she sounded to us like a native, but of course we were not the best of judges.

She was only ten or so years older than we were, yet it was enough of a gap to make us treat her deferentially, as the professor's wife, the role in which she was presented. One evening one of the more outspoken girls asked how she and the professor had happened to meet and marry.

"I was a student here in a program like yours," she said. Her English had a very faint tinge of otherness, not an accent exactly, for she was a native speaker, but a hint that the words and inflections were seldom used, taken out on special occasions like fine linen—crisp and slightly self-conscious. "The professor was doing the seminars, the tours, the whole bit. At the end I . . . just stayed. We got married. That's the story." She smiled ironically and shrugged, the way the girls in our group sometimes smiled and shrugged, as if to imply they possessed more information and wisdom than we men could dream of, and withheld it out of a teasing, challenging perversity. At that instant I saw her as having been one of us, the young and unsettled, rather than as a grown-up, established, foreign sophisticate. She became a person who had taken a risky turn, surprised and perhaps even dismayed her family. Tricked fate, as it were. A palpable illustration that we might do the same.

Often at the end of the seminar the professor would disappear for lengthy telephone calls, or to say goodnight to the children, or on unknown errands, and Janet would sit with us. I thought she was simply fulfilling her duty, till after a while I saw she was genuinely interested. More than interested—on the lookout for something. I don't know how I sensed it: she didn't seem bored with her own life—there was a shimmering animation about her, a sense of being richly present—but she was restless, too; she enjoyed stirring things up and inducing revelation. She would ask questions that coaxed our awkward self-doubts to the surface, and she managed to do this without being rude or overbearing, but by being charming. Once she had made us speak of our uncertainties they seemed no longer awkward but brimming with possibility.

Gradually I became the one she spoke to most often. Looking back, I think perhaps I seemed most in need of being shaken loose, released from the claws of naïveté. We would sit in the glow of the fireplace as she interrogated me like a curious, unconventional aunt from far away. What did I think about my past, did I like my parents,

what were my ambitions, what did I want to find out
about the world?

"How things work," I said hesitantly.

"What things, for instance?"

"Well, cells."

"Cells," she repeated. She got me to talk about a fairly
commonplace senior project I had undertaken in the lab,
involving cross-breeding in fruit flies, and though she was
attentive there was a playful note to her attention, as if,
while these were important matters, we must not take them
too seriously. I found her easy to talk to, but confusing.

One late afternoon I met her in the Borghese Gardens,
where I would often wander on my own, semi-intoxicated
with the mere idea of being where I was. After chatting
for a moment I was about to continue on my way, but she
suggested a coffee. I was impressed with the way she ordered the waiter about in typically imperious Roman fash-
ion, and tossed back the dark brew in one gulp. I expected
we would talk in our usual manner; I was still acting the
boy prepared to be questioned, to indulge my fantasies
in her adult attentiveness. But after a few moments of
this she said, "Don't you have any curiosity about what's
around you? Do you ever feel the need to ask questions?"
I was puzzled. Mired in deference, I had little experience
in talking to adults on equal terms.

"Well, sure. How come you went so far from home?" I
asked.

She laughed. "I came here to get away from people like
you." She spoke in a friendly way, a way that invited
further questions, but in my puzzlement I said nothing.
"From innocence," she added, as if I had urged her on.
"American innocence."

I had an inkling, then, of what she had in mind, for even
the most untried young man senses, if nothing else, a sexual challenge. But I simply couldn't believe it. She went on
to tell me she had grown up on a farm in Nebraska—not

all that far from my own small Minnesota town, yet I doubted that I could ever grow so comfortably urbane. Even after three years I was not quite at ease in my Ivy League college, which I attended thanks to a scholarship. As a matter of fact I am not quite at ease even now.

As she talked that afternoon, she would occasionally touch my arm or wrist. Just before we got up to leave, she let her fingers rest on my arm for an unsettling time. I knew, but was still afraid to trust my instinct. Or my luck, as a college boy would doubtless have put it then.

"Why don't we walk for a while?" she said. "Or are you rushing off to pursue your studies?"

Of course I agreed to walk. By now I was desperate to touch her, my hands were drawing into fists, the blood was rushing through me—all of which she surely knew. But I was afraid. Italians were famously demonstrative, affectionate: if she were simply doing as the Romans do I might be making a shameful mistake. I could end up in trouble, be sent home in disgrace. What would my parents say? It sounds ludicrous now, I know. Young Americans are no longer so ignorant or inept.

"Do you have a girlfriend here yet?" she asked. "An Italian? Or is that all happening within the group?"

"No," I said. "There's very little of that going on, unfortunately. We haven't had a chance to meet too many Italians so far. And we're mostly just friends."

"Just friends," she mocked. "What wholesome young people."

We were walking up toward the Pincio—for the view, she suggested. It was about five o'clock on a March afternoon, still fairly cold. At the top of the hill we stopped to look down at the traffic and hubbub circling the great column in the Piazza del Popolo, and in the distance, in the fading light, the ruins. Hugging her shoulders against the wind, she turned to me in such a teasing way that even a dolt such as I knew I was supposed to kiss her. If before I had feared it might be a disgrace to kiss her, now I knew I would be disgraced if I didn't. And I wanted to very badly anyway.

What followed is easily imagined—how I was initiated into the intrigue of secret meetings and deceptions, how I felt this to be the great adventure of my life (as indeed it was). She was not only a restless woman, I discovered, but a beautiful and rare one. I had hardly noticed her beauty and rarity—I was so predisposed to see her as the professor's wife. Naturally I felt guilty throughout, above all when the professor spent time helping me with a term paper, or when, after the seminars, he said, "Janet, would you bring us the coffee, please?" I would watch her, deft and gracious, the very picture of an elegant faculty wife, serving the coffee without taking any particular notice of me.

Guilty, but also boundlessly thrilled and excited: it was at those moments, in the presence of the group, in the presence of her husband, that I craved her the most. One night I couldn't bear it, and followed her into the kitchen on the pretext of carrying some cups and saucers, to run my hand along her back and hips. She looked over her shoulder as if I were a mad vulgarian, as if our intimate hours were a boy's dream.

"What on earth do you think you're doing?" Like a boy, I quickly drew my hand back. I almost apologized, but I was not that much of a boy anymore. The next day, when we were alone, she said, "That simply isn't how you go about things. You're ruined if you start taking those chances."

"Oh, do you do this often? You sound like you have the routine down pat," I said, seized with jealousy.

"No," she said. "Just once, a few years ago."

"Also a student? Do you specialize?"

"Not a student," she said, and wouldn't say more except, "Don't be nasty, don't spoil everything."

"And will you do it again?"

She laughed. "How can I tell?"

"Why with me?"

"Do you really need to ask?"

"I guess I do."

"I liked you. You seemed the right sort."

"What sort is that?"

"Oh," and she pretended to think it over, or perhaps really did think it over. "Decent. Clever." I was flattered then, but later dismayed. Decent and clever? Not exactly stirring declarations to an ardent lover.

I assumed she must be miserable with the professor: why else would she have sought me out? But she laughed this off as another sign of my conventional ignorance. She said nothing disparaging about him, never talked of him at all, except to answer, when I inevitably asked, that they made love infrequently. I realize by this time how many women say that to their lovers, yet I believe it was true. I believed everything she said—there was such an air of conviction about her—though while she told the truth, it could not have been the whole truth. Possibly she thought I was not ready to hear the whole truth, or possibly, as in my own research, truth can never be told in its entirety.

I asked if she minded being summoned to serve coffee to students week after week and she said not at all, there was no indignity in serving coffee. Besides, it was part of the bargain. What bargain, I wanted to ask, but was too uneasy and suspected she wouldn't answer anyway. Explanation was hardly her style. She liked talking to the students, was all she volunteered; it gave her a chance to speak English.

"But this person who made the bargain, the person you are with him—is that really you?"

"It's no more false than this. I can be any number of people. Don't you find that?" Not a new notion by any means, but the first time I had seen it enacted. "Do you think," she said tauntingly, "that the person you see is the only 'real' me? Do you think there are real and unreal selves?" I had in fact thought so, but from her ironic tone it would have been mortifying to confess it.

I found her a riddle. Later, of course, I would see her as a complex, self-willed woman, and such types tend to be inscrutable to men. But back then she was older than anyone I had ever known, far older than her age—a thirty-one-year-old woman with the mind of an eighty-year-old. It was she who described herself that way, and I came to feel she was right. She lived as though she had seen and assessed everything and had had the time to put it into perspective, and now had very little time left and need answer only to herself.

When the semester ended I scrambled to find a way to stay for the summer. For her. She urged me to stay, but I didn't need much urging. The professor was going to Holland and Germany for several months to do research. I managed to get a job as a waiter in a café. I knew enough Italian, by then, to take the imperiously snapped orders. We made love whenever we could, when the children were napping, or late at night, or weekends when Janet could leave them with her in-laws. However unique and indescribable it felt to me, our love clearly belonged to a well-documented genre: brief, heedless, intense, and transforming. But my story is not about the loss of innocence or the discovery—it felt like the invention—of passion, or about loving in an unidealistic, futureless, encapsulated, carnal way, which may be what loss of innocence is. The real story takes place two decades later.

———

After I returned home and finished college I was drafted, as expected. I spent two months in Vietnam surviving in a way I could not in a million years recount. In truth I have done all I can to forget it. I was wounded early on, in the shoulder, and luckily spent the rest of my time at a desk. I seldom watched the news reports or read the papers about it, afterward. I was no soldier and no activist. I am not interested in politics but in science. I know how irresponsible that sounds—I have often been lectured about it. And when I am I say nothing, just remind myself that I work, however marginally, on a cure for cancer: that should be enough.

Graduate studies in science are among the most laborious and demanding: you can get to be thirty or more before you assume a real position, draw a respectable paycheck and feel like an adult. Most of the students came from more comfortable backgrounds than mine. My family had a hard time figuring out why, in my late twenties and after so many years in school, I was still writing a dissertation and earning a workman's wage. They said that with the same efforts I might have gone to medical school and become a prosperous doctor. It wasn't their fault that they couldn't see how specific my interests were. When I was finally done I wanted some ease. I wanted not to have to account for myself all the time. I married a woman with whom that would be possible. A nurse: I met her in the emergency room when I was badly bruised hitting the chain-link fence as I reached for an impossibly high ball.

She was, and is, a stocky, pretty, able woman with pale brown, boyishly cut hair. I loved her and still do, even if it is not the kind of love pictured in books or films, or that I knew with Janet. It is love all the same, and arguably stronger than what I knew with Janet, possessing a structure and endurance. This sounds unfair to my wife, perhaps, now that I see it set down so baldly, and yet she enjoys a good life. We have our children and our house and our work and our friends, and we sleep close together at night still.

Several months ago, in an Italian scientific journal, I came across a series of articles on migratory cells. With my dregs of Italian I could see they might be crucial to my research, but returning to a long-lost language is not, alas, like riding a bicycle, where no matter how long ago, they say, you remember how. A colleague suggested I call the Romance Languages Department: they could send over a graduate student to translate, who would be glad of the extra money. The secretary called back promptly to say she had just the person, a very bright Italian student who was bilingual—her mother was British or American or something—besides being punctual, reliable, and so forth. I was rushing to class and didn't ask her name, just said to send her over the next morning during my office hours. I didn't really think of her as a person at all, then. I was excited about what I might learn and couldn't wait to see the translation. The student was merely a step on the way to satisfying my curiosity.

She arrived promptly at ten: tall, slim, pale, and auburn-haired, wearing a soft gray wool skirt, a green sweater, and leather boots, not the usual jeans and sweatshirt uniform. She wanted to appear professional, I thought. Her manner was unstudentlike as well. Students are usually shy and fumbling or else excessively candid and enthusiastic, which comes to the same thing. This one seemed reserved, not shy: she presented herself in an economical way, just as much as necessary for the purpose. All in all, she was extremely self-possessed.

"I've come about the translation work," she said, and announced her name. Francesca. The last name—well of course that is obvious by this time. Life, like science, is full of the coincidences that unleash discovery.

I was glad to be seated, because I might have toppled over. I had the oddest sense that my face was escaping me, I was losing control over it. I felt a jumble of wonderment, panic, curiosity—I had no idea what might be happening on the surface. I tried to smile and be polite, but for all I knew I looked stunned.

How could I be sure so quickly? The name, as I have said, was unusual even for Mediterranean names with their syllabic frills and furbelows. There couldn't be many with that name. Still, I needed to be absolutely certain.

"I spent some time in Rome when I was a student." I tried to sound casual, though my mind teemed with memories and frantic calculations. I hoped my worst suspicion wasn't so, and yet I hoped it was. "On an art history program."

"Really," she said mildly.

What did I expect? Thousands must have done the same. I made myself stumble on. "One of my professors had your name. His first name was Federico."

She showed no great surprise. "That's my father. He's a professor of art history."

"Is that so?" Now it was legitimate to sound a bit excited, so my feelings had some release. "Isn't that a coincidence! I knew both your parents. They used to have the students over all the time. That little street near the Piazza Navona. Did you grow up there?"

"Yes, I remember the students. They were coming over until quite recently." She smiled indulgently, as if hosting American students was a lovable eccentricity of her quaint parents.

"What a coincidence!" I said again.

"Well, really not that strange. They must have entertained hundreds of American students. What did you think of them, my parents, that is?"

That sort of abrupt slashing through pleasantries was exactly her mother's style and unsettled me for an instant, like hearing the rustlings of a ghost. But I was not a boy now; I had had the beneficent experience of her mother. "I found them wonderful people. They made us feel so at home, especially your mother. How is your mother?"

"Mother died last fall." She looked down to get away from me. This was private, delicate territory. She was still grieving. And I, I could not even tell what I was feeling, apart from grim surprise and a pressing warmth behind my eyes. I fended it off. I needed all my forces just to speak casually to the girl. I was not permitted to express anything out of the ordinary. I would take the news home with me, for later. "I'm so sorry. She must have been still relatively young, as I remember. What—what was it?"

"It's all right, you can ask. She had cancer. Lymphoma."

"Ah."

"It was pretty quick. She wasn't sick very long."

"And you—" I felt slightly dizzy and gripped the edge of the desk to anchor myself. "I wonder if you were one of the little girls I used to see playing? I don't think there was a Francesca, though. One was Elsa, I remember. Rosa?"

"Very good." She smiled as though I were a clever child. "There's Elsa and Rosalia, then me, then Pietro—he's two years younger."

"I see. Well, I was there in 'sixty-six . . ."

"A year too soon for me. I was twenty-three just last week, in fact."

"April."

"April, yes." She frowned ironically, then laughed. The eyes, green and witty, were her mother's. "Why, do you follow astrology, like your former president? Americans are so amusing sometimes. The cruelest month, as one of your poets says."

If they know nothing else, I have found, the students all know that line; in that respect, she was generic. Then I realized her knowledge would be more than superficial: my daughter was a student of literature. For as I feared and hoped, I was looking at my own daughter. I wanted to leap up and embrace her. I wanted to do all sorts of things at once, laugh, weep, mourn her mother, find out about the family, even reveal myself. For a moment I thought I might do this—not right away, but some day in the future. But only for a moment.

Still, could I be sure? one may ask. Oh, I was sure. Even if the dates hadn't worked out, even if it weren't true that Janet rarely made love with the professor, this girl was mine. I could see it. She had my coloring. My hair, before it faded and started going gray. My family's body, tall and narrow and energetic, though her movements had an un-American mellowness. She reminded me of my mother and my older sister. I wondered if they would notice, were they to see her. Could I ever manage to introduce her? How could I explain her? Yet all the while I knew this would never come to pass. I wouldn't mind shocking my family at this point, but I could not shock her, Francesca. She had her father—she didn't need another.

"No," I laughed. "I don't follow astrology. In your mother's case April was a lucky month, I'd say. And how is your father?"

She passed over my compliment. "He's fine. He just re-tired from the university but he still writes papers. Of course it was terrible for him, my mother . . . They were so devoted. So close. You must have noticed. But he has lots of friends. And my sisters live nearby and keep an eye on him. My brother is in school at Berkeley. We both flew back when Mother was sick. Well, you don't need to hear all this. Would you like to tell me about the translation?"

"No, no, I really do want to hear. I remember them so vividly."

She smiled. "There's nothing more to tell."

"When you write will you give him my regards?"

"Sure. But there were so many, you know . . . The house was like a—a port of call. My mother was con-stantly serving them coffee and listening to their prob-lems. I guess you know."

"Yes." I couldn't stop staring at her, trying to find traces of my children, my other children. She was beautiful in a way it took a while to appreciate, even more so than her mother, whom she did not resemble except for the eyes and the cool, self-possessed manner. Like Janet's, her statements were assertions, with a tinge of irony.

She was also, like Janet, decisively, provocatively polite. "About the translation . . .," she prompted.

"It's only natural," I mused, "that this should be an amazing coincidence for me, while for you . . . I mean, to come upon an old acquaintance of your parents, all the way across the ocean—no big deal, right?"

"On the contrary, it's a pleasure to meet you."

What I felt at that moment was pride, I must admit. Paternal pride. Few Americans of twenty-three would speak with such aplomb. And her speech was not diluted with the nervous, meaningless tics, the "likes" or "you knows" that disjointed the talk of even the brightest students. Well, God knows I had had nothing to do with it. Credit her mother. "But it can't be quite the same pleasure."

"Nothing is quite the same as anything else, is it?"

"How true." I laughed faintly. "Well, let me tell you what I need to have done." I showed her the articles. "Do you think you'll have trouble with the technical terms?"

She didn't answer right away, but leafed through the pages. "I don't think so. It's the technical terms that are similar in both languages. Besides, that's what dictionaries are for, aren't they?" She gave me a rather impish grin, and suddenly I felt something new stirring in the room. I was grown now—it no longer took me weeks to identify it. The girl, I was almost sure, was flirting with me. She had sensed my interest and was responding. I would have to be more careful.

"It's about cancer cells."

"So I see."

"I hope that's not—I mean, will it upset you?"

She gazed at me as her mother used to, as if I were ludicrously inept. "I've already had the reality. There's not much the words can add."

"Yes, I see. I'm sorry. So, when do you think you can have this ready? Is three weeks too soon?"

"No, that's all right."

I arranged to pay her fifteen dollars an hour, which she seemed to find generous. "Then we're all set, uh—do you mind if I call you Francesca?"

Again she smiled coolly. "What else?"

"Well, I might call you Signorina." I didn't mean to encourage her but couldn't help myself. I was at a loss. I only wanted to get closer to her, befriend her.

"I don't think we have to be quite that formal. Professor." This time there was no doubt. She flung her tweed coat over her shoulders and was gone.

I locked the door, then sat down, bent my head to the desk, and allowed myself my grief. It could not wait to be taken home. And nothing about Janet belonged at home.

When at last I looked up I thought of her, Francesca, again. My daughter. I had three fine, healthy sons: nine, twelve, and fourteen. I had renounced—my wife and I had, I should say—the prospect of a daughter long ago, without any great pangs. Yet how luscious the idea seemed, now that I had seen her. Had she been in my department I might have invited her over, taken an interest and helped her with her work. Even so, mightn't I befriend her through the translation, ask her over as a kind gesture to a foreign student, make her part of the family? I was aware that faculty wives didn't appreciate their husbands' befriending beautiful students, and in the couple of cases I had observed, their lack of enthusiasm was borne out by the facts. My wife was not particularly suspicious or jealous: I had never given her reason to be. How would she react to Francesca? I might tell her the truth (though not the whole truth): she was the daughter of people who had been hospitable to me in Rome years ago and I wanted to return the favor. But I knew myself: I could not live comfortably with the pretense.

Besides, my wife knows me too, in that unnerving way that wives do. She knows, for instance, that I am less interested in finding a cure for cancer than in charting the erratic paths of the cells or unraveling the logic that makes them travel and hide, erupt and masquerade. At the university hospital—she is head nurse of the intensive care unit—she sees dying patients every day. She respects my research, yet I have a feeling she finds it somewhat abstract and irrelevant. She finds me abstracted, too—though I hope not irrelevant. Maybe, in her plainspoken way, she sees the same ingenuousness Janet found so amusing. Maybe it has never fallen away with age, only transmuted into what Americans dignify with the term *absentmindedness*. I suppose I am absent, in a sense, from my life. I was present with Janet—as who could not be?—and I am present in the laboratory, and often with my sons. Otherwise I suppose I hold myself in abeyance, I don't know why, or for what. I don't mean any harm that I know of. I only feel vague. I am not disappointed with my life; sometimes it feels better than I expected. There was a period, after we had been married a few years and had our first child, when my wife accused me of being disappointed and having cooled, but I denied that, and soon she stopped mentioning it. She finds great satisfaction in her work as well as in the boys, and we get on companionably. I am grateful we never had the turbulence of divorce I have seen disrupt and sometimes destroy the lives of friends and colleagues.

———

Though the Romance Languages Department is in the building across the lawn from mine, I had never noticed Francesca before. Now I saw her everywhere—lounging on the front steps; in the gym, where I played racquetball and she swam; in the local drugstore; in the faculty club, where she was eating with, apparently, some boisterously entertaining young instructors from Romance Languages. Each time, she came up to greet me with her mother's provocative, ambiguous tone. And I responded. She was my daughter: how could I be aloof with her? I was inexpressibly touched to see she liked me, was even drawn to me. I am a pleasant-mannered, nice-looking man, but don't flatter myself that I cut a dashing figure. Something more obscure drew her. I felt as I do in the lab when I draw near to the heart of the mystery—troubled and excited, and though it is where I want to be, I want also to draw back.

I tried to keep a proper distance: I would ask how the translation was going, and she would say fine. Once, coming out of the library, she said she was stopping for coffee, did I want to join her? Naturally I did—I wanted any chance to be near her.

She ordered an espresso and tossed it back in one gulp. She was in her first year of graduate work, she told me. She had gotten her undergraduate degree from Harvard. Harvard! She was studying comparative literature; she had learned French in school and, with her Italian, found Spanish a breeze. German was more difficult. She wasn't sure what she would write her dissertation on—at the moment she was fascinated by the Latin American novelists, but she had a new enthusiasm every month, she said with a self-mocking smile. "Intellectually fickle is what I am, I guess," and she waved regally for another coffee.

I said very little, just basked in her presence. In retrospect, I see I must have appeared entranced, as I truly was. I kept thinking how delightful and eager she was, and how she would never know the truth about herself. Unless Janet had told her, and she, Francesca, was playing some sly game of privileged information. No, knowing Janet, that was inconceivable.

"And what about you, Professor," she said with a droll glance. "I can see from the articles what you're interested in, but what else? Are you married?"

"Yes." I told her about my wife and children. I even pulled pictures from my wallet to show her, and while she said all the proper things—What handsome boys!—she seemed a trifle daunted. I wanted so badly to tell her she was looking at her brothers. Half-brothers. "Are you sure your mother never mentioned me? I know there were lots of students but I—well, I must confess I had a bit of a crush on her."

"Is that so?" Francesca gave her ironic smile. "You were hardly the only one. She was Queen of the Students. She loved it. She was going strong well into her fifties, until the end. Yes, she broke quite a few hearts."

"Oh, but not really— You're not saying that—"

"Of course not!" With all her sophistication, she seemed shocked, as children are invariably shocked at their parents' adventures. "They were kids to her. She and my father used to joke about them after they left. He would guess which ones liked her and she would correct him. I remember them laughing over their coffee. They could never agree on which ones."

"I see."

"What do you mean, you see? What on earth does that mean?"

"I don't know, it's just something to say when you don't know what else to say."

"Don't worry, it wasn't malicious laughter. They loved being around the students. They said it kept them young."

I was newly disturbed when we parted. So close, she had said the very first day. So devoted. But I couldn't lose myself in brooding all over again, at this late date. I would understand no better, only feel more pain. What did it matter now? She was dead. The boy I had been was as good as dead. Except for Francesca, that is.

A few days later she turned up in my office, very businesslike, with the translation. I thanked her and made a note to have the secretary send her a check. She said to contact her if there were any problems with the text, and wrote her phone number on a slip of paper.

"Do you live in the dorms?"

"No, I'm a grad student, remember? I'm too old for the dorms. I have an apartment across campus."

"I see."

"Ah," she laughed, "there you go again. Seventy-four Crabtree Street, if that's what 'I see' meant this time."

"No, it didn't, actually."

"I see," she said, still smiling, taunting. There are countless rules, nowadays, regarding the most tenuous sexual innuendos chanced by professors. One has to be wary, even someone like me who has never chanced anything of the kind. No rules for the opposite, I thought wryly.

"Do you have a boyfriend?" It was fatherly interest—I hoped she would say yes. I could invite them over together. It would be easier for me, as well as for my wife.

To my surprise, her face turned sober. Younger. "There's someone back in Rome I've known a long time, and I always thought . . . But now I'm not sure anymore."

"You mean someone from before college? But you were so young."

"Well, yes. We both knew there might be other people. We're far apart and I'm not . . . shy that way—" She paused and gave me the oddest look, half-earnest, half-coy, utterly young, yet I had seen enough of her, not to mention her mother, to know it was also maddeningly canny. Economical as ever, she was accomplishing a great deal at once. "Still, there was some understanding . . . When I went back last fall, when Mother died, we spent a lot of time together. And at a time like that, when someone is close to you and acts kind, you tend to accept what they do for you, and then they think . . . Do you know what I mean?"

"I think so."

"But now I wonder. I feel it would be retreating, in a way. From I don't know what. From life. I see people around and I'm, well, interested, what's wrong with saying it? Everybody is. Why should I have to hold back because I promised things when I was almost a child and didn't know any better? And yet he's a friend of the family, he's— Oh, look, I'm sorry. Why on earth would you want to listen to all this? I've got to be going."

"No, really, I am interested."

"You are? Why?"

"I just am. I guess because I knew your parents, and, well, you're such a lovely young woman."

She mistook my words again, willfully, it seemed, and as easily as slipping out of a dress, she slipped out of her earnest, girlish mode. I was sorry, for I loved hearing it, loved her talking to me as if I might be a father. A father figure, anyway.

"Indeed," was all she said. She sounded like her mother. I could see how she might be irresistible.

"Ah, indeed. That's hardly better than 'I see,'" I teased.

"You're right. What else can I say to a mixed message?"

"Mixed message? Not at all. I meant just what I said. Look, you really must come over for dinner one night, meet my family."

"Meet your family?" She looked dubious. "Well, thank you. That's very kind. Do you want to check it out with your wife first, maybe?"

"I'll see what night is convenient and let you know. She works some nights. And thanks again for getting this to me so promptly, Francesca."

———

I told my wife about the translation. I told her the almost unbelievable coincidence of the translator being the daughter of a couple who had been hospitable to me in

Rome when I was a student. I told her I needed to go over some small points in the articles with the girl, and would like to invite her for dinner one night, partly out of gratitude to her parents and partly to be kind: her mother had died recently. I had never been duplicitous with my wife in this way, but found it remarkably easy. It was what Janet and I had had to do, with her husband, her baby-sitter, my fellow students. Like riding a bicycle indeed. I even remembered it was not necessary or propitious to add lies, such as that Francesca seemed lonely and found it hard to make friends, and so on. My wife was struck by the coincidence. OK, she said, how about Friday night?

Ah, she had many guises, my old-world young daughter did. She performed graciously the role of foreign student enjoying the hospitality of kind Americans. She praised the food, bantered easily with the boys, helped clear the table, and answered with tact and patience all the usual questions asked of foreigners, comparing life abroad and in the States. After dinner, in my study, we went over a few small points in the translation. I saw I could relax: she was quite professional as, of course, was I. I remembered how her mother had chilled my caresses when the professor and the students were in the next room.

When we returned to the living room the boys had gone upstairs and my wife was curled up in the easy chair, reading the paper. I said I would drive Francesca home. She and my wife exchanged the customary thank-you's and hopes to meet again. They didn't kiss as some women do even on first meeting—neither was expansive enough for that—but the warmth between them seemed genuine.

"Crabtree, was it?" I said in the car.

"Ah, you remembered."

"It's nothing special. I have a good memory for details."

"Oh. Well, you have a very nice family. I enjoyed meeting them. You must be quite pleased with yourself." The lower part of her face was buried in her scarf; she was peering out at me sideways.

"I'm pleased, yes, I suppose so."

"Your wife is a good cook, too."

"Yes."

"Did you accomplish what you hoped from the evening, then?"

"I had no specific hopes. I thought it went nicely. Why, were you disturbed about anything?"

"Not at all, it was lovely." She was silent for the rest of the short ride, except, near the end, to point out the house, an old-fashioned three-story frame house divided into apartments, with an ample porch.

"I'd invite you to sit on the porch for a while, but it's too cold."

"Freezing for this time of year," I said. "Anyway, I should get back."

"Yes, you should. Definitely."

"I'm very sorry you're irritated. I can't explain."

"There's nothing to explain. It's not too complex to understand."

"Please don't be angry, Francesca."

"Oh, all right." She gave a bit of a laugh, and again seemed to shake off the mood as easily as a dress. "I'll see you around." And she laid her hand on my arm, just the barest touch.

"Yes. Good night. Thanks again for the translation. You did a terrific job."

"Good night." She leaned over and kissed me very lightly and swiftly on the lips. It was nothing really, no more than a fleeting feathery brush, but then she waited. I was supposed to kiss her back. And maybe it would have been better if I had—just once, and properly, with ardor: then she could have kept her illusion that, like many a timid professor, I wanted her but didn't dare risk my domestic peace. A benign, bittersweet illusion, not one of the noxious kinds. Better than my sitting there unmoving and righteous. Yes, I suppose I did the wrong thing. I suppose it was a disgrace not to kiss her, but I feared the disgrace, in my own eyes, of kissing her even once. Besides, I didn't want to kiss her. I wanted to kiss her mother.

Back home, my wife was still reading the paper in the easy chair. "That was quick," she said.

"She doesn't live far."

"Still, I thought you might take longer."

I threw my coat on a chair and headed for the stairs. I was utterly exhausted.

"There's something between you and that girl, isn't there?"

I stopped on the third stair and faced her. "Nothing of the kind. How could you think that?"

"I'm not wrong. Maybe nothing yet. Maybe you don't even know it yourself yet, but there's something."

"You don't know how wrong you are. It's out of the question. I'm surprised you should even suggest it."

"You should be surprised by me once in a while."

"That may be. That may be. But this is inconceivable."

"All right, never mind then," she said, and turned back to her paper.

She didn't speak of it anymore, but she thinks it.

I have never invited Francesca home again. I see her on campus all the time. I watch her from afar and try to avoid coming face to face, for when I do she is cool. To talk to her, to ask her to lunch, which is what I long to do—simply to sit across from her and look at her—would be unfair. In a couple of years, when she finishes her studies, she will go away, and I will be relieved and bereft, never knowing whether she goes home to marry her childhood sweetheart (unlikely, I'd say) or falls in love with someone new, maybe an American. It's not inconceivable that I could run into her somewhere in twenty years, and then will she smilingly, ironically recall how she once had a slight crush on me, very slight, just a vague sense there might be something between us—but I wouldn't give it half a chance? Would it be possible to tell her then? Or even worse than now?

All this might happen, unless something changes erratically in me and I do what she wishes and my wife suspects. I believe I am incapable of that, but I know some organisms are capable of the most unpredictable, riotous, malign behavior. I hope I am not. ⁊

LYNNE SHARON SCHWARTZ's most recent novel *Leaving Brooklyn* was nominated for the 1990 PEN Faulkner Award for Fiction. Her earlier books include the novels *Disturbances in the Field*, *Rough Strife*, and *Balancing Acts* and two collections of stories *Acquainted With the Night* and *The Melting Pot and Other Subversive Stories*. Her translation from Italian of Liana Millu's *Smoke Over Birkenau* received the 1991 PEN Renato Poggioli Award for Translation.

DAGOBERTO GILB

TRUCK

In the center of the carpenter's shop was the table saw. As always, or almost, Martínez was holding a piece of wood against the fence, his straw cowboy hat a little low on his forehead, a cigarette slanted out the right side of his mouth, his eyes slit onto a bevel cut he was guiding through. A few of the men, carpenters and laborers, had hopped up and sat on the work table which L-ed two walls. Others stood near the radial arm saw, a couple leaned against the drill press. Two more men hovered near Martínez, so full of admiration their expressions verged on love. Since Martínez had once been employed in a cabinet shop, he was the star of the show, the man called on for the fine jobs, when patience and delicacy were more important than speed and strength. These two men near him were especially impressed by his skill.

The table saw was loud, even louder when it was cutting, and nobody bothered much about talking with it engaged. But when the power was shut off and the motor wound down, the contrasting silence was dramatic. Modesty being another of Martínez's virtues, he liked to take the hushed moment at the center of the shop to remark on his just-finished product with self-deprecation.

"It'll have to do," he pronounced, the cigarette between

American Short Fiction, Volume 2, Number 7, Fall 1992
© *1992 Dagoberto Gilb*

his lips waving up and down with each syllable. He held the cut piece there, eyeballing the length as he savored a drag off the unfiltered butt.

Blondie, the foreman, known jokingly as el mero güero, was at his wooden desk at another corner of the shop. In fact his blond hair was mostly gray. "Moya," he called, waving Alex over. Carlos Davis followed a step behind.

"You wanna buy it?" Blondie asked. He liked Alex. "It's almost new."

"It's a .357 Magnum?" Alex asked. Carlos was big-eyed over Alex's shoulder.

"Forty-four Magnum. If you don't know the difference, you don't know."

"Can I see it?" Carlos asked.

Blondie's head went back and his eyebrows lifted, meaning no way. He didn't need to respond with words, and he seldom used them, a result, probably, of his not knowing any Spanish and working with so many men who knew so little English. He'd worked for the city over twenty years, and this was his last week. He handed the pistol to Alex. He liked Alex, liked his work, but he didn't trust Carlos. A few of the other men wandered over, including Martínez.

"I guess not," Alex told him as he babied it in his hands. "Sure wouldn't want it aimed at me."

Martínez—nobody used his first name—reached for the gun, and Alex passed it on. "Go right through two or three walls, I hear," he said. "Puts a hole in the man the size of a football, I hear."

Blondie nodded, indifferent to the information. "Good protection," he said. "I just wanna sell it."

"Not today," Alex apologized.

"I own a Remington shotgun," Martínez said. "It'll put a hole in the right places, too."

"Yeah, well . . ." Blondie stared back at his desk, at a pile of work requisitions. "This one's for you," he told Alex. "A partition at the Armijo Center."

"Just me and Carlos?"

Blondie nodded. Then he shook some keys off the desk. "I'm going ahead and giving you this truck." It was the truck the shop had been promised a year earlier but had just got the week before. If Blondie hadn't retired, it would've been his to drive home. The new foreman didn't need one because he already had one.

Alex could feel Martínez's sigh of disapproval. He'd spend the rest of the day talking about what a mistake this was, how one of the other carpenters deserved it more.

"One thing," Blondie said, pulling the hand with the keys back to keep Alex's attention. He glanced over at Martínez, who was listening closer than he pretended, before he spoke. "Well, you know, or you should by now."

———

After he and Carlos slid plywood and two-by-fours onto the bed of the truck, Alex picked up a skilsaw and a cord and some nails, then loaded them and his toolbox. It was a long drive from the city's yard in the rural Lower Valley to the Segundo Barrio. Alex, who was always in a hurry, was about to get on I-10. "N'hombre!" Carlos told him. "Go the long ways, make it happen slow." He'd dragged out the last word like he was talking about sex. Alex grinned and nodded and cruised North Loop, whiffing the damp smell of horses.

Carlos was excited about being in the truck—maybe the newest auto he'd ever been in, besides a police car, and it was close to two years old. "You see how I told you?" he said. "I told you about Blondie, how he'd listen. He knows how you're the best carpenter. He knows. He knows about that metiche Martínez, too, how he talks pedo behind your back . . ."

"Forget about it, man," Alex said, cutting him short. "Let's forget about that dude."

Carlos had a habit of going too far, making fights. Not that he wasn't right about Martínez. And Blondie did honor Alex with one of the trucks—Urquidi drove the one-ton for the large jobs which most of the men went to, but now he and Martínez would be treated as equals for the smaller, two-man jobs. Still, Carlos exaggerated, just like he did about what a great carpenter Alex was. His exaggerations confused Alex as much as his confessions, like the one about stealing from the shop. A block plane, a Phillips screwdriver, some needle-nose pliers. Things did get lost, and probably other men had taken a tool or two. Carlos wasn't exactly wrong about this. But if Alex wasn't sure it wasn't exactly right either, he didn't say so. He couldn't resist the admiration, seeming smart, or skilled, or whatever it was Carlos saw in him, and he didn't want to be a disappointment. And then, even though he was eight years older than Carlos, who was twenty, Alex carried a private respect for him. Alex might stand up and say he could hold his own, but Carlos had been raised real tough and done real bad, and that, like having been to war, was a strength that was always veiled and mysterious, envied by those who grew up on the easier side of the highway. All Alex had done to be this great carpenter was work for his cousin's construction company. He wanted this city job because it was steady—he was married and the father of two daughters, one not even a year old. It was Carlos's first job ever.

Carlos had grown up on Seventh Street. He came up behind one of the turquoise-framed screen doors, with only one light bulb, in that gray brick building, its seventy-year-old lintels and thresholds tilted and sagging, the building across the street from the one painted sapphire, next to the ruby one, a block away from the one whose each apartment was a swath of brilliant Mexican color—the whole street woven with shades as bold and ornate

and warm as an Indian blanket. Across the street from the
Armijo Center, at the Boy's Club, Carlos stabbed a dude
when he was eleven. Across from there, under the mural
of Che Guevara, where all those gang placazos are sprayed
in black, he soaked red bandannas, shut his eyes, and
sniffed until his mind floated away like in a light wind.

"That's some stupid shit," Alex told him. "Make your
brains turn to hamburger."

"Already I know now," Carlos said, serious, "but I
didn't then." His lips bent sarcastically. "If they turned into
tacos, that'd be something else, eh?"

Alex had been driving real slow down the street listening to Carlos, even went past the Armijo by a couple of
blocks before he U-turned around.

"Park in the front, güey," Carlos said. "You got the city
sign on the side. I wanna show off for my bros."

"It's a loading zone." Alex parked in the lot beside the
building. He didn't want to mess up. That's what Blondie
had meant: Martínez was behind the scenes saying how
Alex was no better a carpenter than Carlos was his helper.
"My grandma could do as well, and she's got cataracts,"
was how he'd say it. That the two got along was evidence
of even fewer skills, since Martínez especially didn't like
Carlos. The truck was Blondie's way of backing Alex.

Carlos shook his head displeased, pissed off that he
didn't get his way. "It'd be *bad* parking out in the front like
we own the place."

"We ain't rock stars driving a limousine," Alex said, at
times like this wondering why he ever tried to work with
the guy.

While Alex went through the glass front doors, Carlos
hung back, doing a slow, unhappy strut outside in his chi-
nos and white T-shirt. But once he did push the doors,
too, and saw nobody else was around, he quickened his
pace and dropped the attitude. They unloaded the material

and tools and even flirted with the secretary while they worked—she was married, but she was all right. They built a partition to close off a small, lockable room for basketballs and pool sticks, ping-pong paddles, and the like. They didn't hang the door because it wouldn't be available until next week, but framed and plumbed and anchored and sheeted the wall with plywood, even fixed a couple of other things the secretary pointed out. All of it was done in three hours. Alex *was* fast, especially compared to the other city carpenters. It was all they were expected to do that day.

"Fucking Martínez," Carlos said out on the hardwood basketball courts. "That old dude would still be chopping the tree or some shit. His camaradas would be right at his culo. Oh, Mr. Mar-*tí*-nez, you do it so *good*. Maybe he'd still be hitting on a nail. Tac. Tac. Tac. Fucking put a dude to sleep, like to dead."

Alex had borrowed one of the basketballs. He'd played on his high-school basketball team, once in a while on the asphalt courts on the grounds of Austin High School with some old friends—he was shooting better now than he did back then, and he'd been good in high school.

"Andale, güey!" Carlos was shaking his head under the hoop. "What don't you do good?"

Alex was feeling fine because of his play, and of course the compliment helped. So fine it made him think of those things he didn't do anymore, that he'd left behind. He'd been doing right and that wasn't wrong. But he'd missed out, too. He didn't get to shoot hoops often enough, and he'd forgotten how much fun it was messing around for no reason when—maybe even *because*—he knew he should be doing something better. All his girlfriends were because he made baskets. His wife, who was the best-looking, sweetest girl he met in high school, first smiled at him because the ball swung in the net.

"Let's go to lunch," he said.

"Let's get some beer," Carlos suggested.

"Let's go to lunch and get beer, too," Alex said.

———

They went down the street to the Jalisco Cafe and ordered the special and two beers each. It was still real early, and Alex didn't think it was a good idea to go back to the Armijo with nothing to do.

"Maybe we should just go back to the shop," Alex said.

"N'hombre! We ain't got nothing there. Better we do nothing here. How am I not right?"

It was one of these subjects that Alex didn't feel like arguing about. And Carlos was right—if they went back, they'd have to sit around bored, look for Blondie who probably wouldn't be around, even chance having to explain themselves if someone bigger came by.

Carlos told Alex about a shade tree they could park under, but first he made him stop at Mena's Bakery. Alex assumed it was for some cigarettes. Instead, Carlos came out with two quarts of beer.

"Are you crazy?" Alex said.

"Yessir, I am the crazy dude, at your service." Carlos unscrewed the cap from one and passed it to Alex. He was already having fun.

"We can't do this," Alex said.

Carlos put on his cholo slouch, his head drooping sideways and back. "It's not chiva, not even mota. It's not nothing, güey, just some *beer*."

Alex shook off his worry. He even felt ashamed for being afraid to do something as harmless as this. What kind of man was he becoming? It was no big deal. Who couldn't handle a little beer? And once he settled down and relaxed, he even liked it.

They kicked back under the shade tree for over an hour, then agreed to drive a long route back.

"Over there," Carlos said. Alex stopped the truck by a small grocery on Alameda. Carlos took a five from Alex for the peanuts that would disguise their breath.

He came back with a cocky smile and two more quarts of beer.

"No way, man," said Alex. "We're just going back. We can't walk in there after we drank these."

"I got the peanuts. And these were on sale." Carlos opened his. "Those dudes won't see nothing different in *this* dude."

Alex fought off his impulses at first, even criticized himself again. Then Alex went ahead and opened his and drank and started enjoying himself—not quite like Carlos, who was chugging the bottle in a hurry. But Alex slipped into such a calm about it he drove with his mind on all kinds of things he'd wanted to do that he'd forgotten about, and he drove not thinking of much else other than this until he realized he'd driven too far, way east of the city complex. He both laughed and got mad at this lapse, looked both in front and in the rearview mirror. No cars were coming, and he turned left into the empty field on the other side of the street to turn around.

———

"What a stupid move, güey," Carlos said, irritated. He was more drunk than Alex. He was a sure bust—everybody would see him and know. "That pinche Martínez is gonna be out here to get us and be laughing in our face. What the fuck you do this for?"

They'd tried everything to get it out, but half the tire had dug itself into the sand. They'd tried putting rocks under it, chunks of wood. The tire spun, spraying sandy dirt.

"We ain't gonna get this truck no more," Carlos complained. "You lost us this truck."

Alex didn't disagree, or argue, or offer a word in defense. Like Martínez, Carlos was far away. Alex felt his feet leaving the ground, his arms cocking, the ball rolling off his fingers. As it spun away, arced, the touch of the ball stayed with him, and he felt the pleasure of it stretching the net, and clinging—a long time or short, depending on how he'd remember this moment, just like a first kiss. ✒

DAGOBERTO GILB is a short-story writer and novelist who lives in El Paso, Texas. He is a recipient of a 1992 National Endowment for the Arts Fellowship in Creative Writing. His story "The Death Mask of Pancho Villa" was published in *American Short Fiction* Number 1, Spring 1991.

THE NEW HOUSE

*D*ana Ingles had been promised
that he could go to New Orleans and start school the year
he was twelve. "Twelve is the magic number," said his
father, "if you can straighten out." His father and Nana
(his mother's mother) were trying to help him to be nor-
mal so that he could leave the place and attend the Holy
Name of Jesus in the city.

"Don't hang at the window," his father said, "amazed
that the sun comes up behind the cemetery. It always does.
Or for that matter that it sets over the river. The same sun,
same cemetery, same river. This is the hill country of
southern Mississippi."

According to Nana he was a wise and obedient boy, and
nothing would phase him at Holy Name. "You've been
hearing about Jesus all your life, and He will be there the
same as here."

It all fitted in. He had been to the school once, taken
there by his mother to register. They sent him up some
carved steps to the principal's office. There was a stained
glass window on the landing, very high, with some clouds
and a bright sheep. And there He stood with a shepherd's
crook—it was Jesus all right, Holy Name thereof.

"Don't live in your imagination," his father counseled.

"Look where it's got me. You have had an idyllic child-hood here with Nana and me, read to from the world's great literature. So let's not make a fuss over school. Down there you'll get some math, French, a smattering of it, group experience. Nothing important really."

Nana, standing by with his father's breakfast tray, nod-ded in agreement. She had vertical lines on her upper lip with two ugly white hairs she always said to remind her to pluck out. "The land," she said, "this house, everything will be here when you get back."

Her comment seemed to stir his father up. "Have I ever alienated one acre of this place?" he asked, looking at them defiantly. "Well then. Your duty is to have children, teach them the Faith, keep us going."

Nana explained when they were out of earshot that Papa deserved a lot of credit for not giving in to sorrow over his older son's death. The sacrifice to continue living must al-ways be remembered.

———

His father usually had a morning headache over his right eye. A bad sign, he said, if you listen to Hippocrates. He could barely choke down the half grapefruit and his ome-let, with Nana insisting. Then, after a bath and coming up the hall shaking in his robe, he would get dressed to go to the cemetery. First maybe a test to gauge the young man's power of observation. "Say you're in the dining room, fac-ing the sideboard, where is my father's portrait in relation to his father's?"

The right answer called for a Coke. Then the dog had to be fed, a duty suitable for a young person. Fella, the collie, as quiet and numb as the morning fog, accepted its cornbread and gravy without enthusiasm. After limping round the fig tree Fella would come back in and collapse on the blue hooked rug behind the stove. For the present life might be wearisome, but in the future he would crack

the whip with dominion over everything, would have eager dogs, on their toes to obey.

Nobody was ever quite ready for the dash to the cemetery. Nana had to find the isinglass copy of the prayer for
the dead and give Papa his beads. It was a standing order
that flowers be snatched from wherever they grew around
the house. Pink Perfections in January from the towering
camellia by the front porch, then Naked Ladies, amaryllis,
that popped up leafless around the summer kitchen. The
race was to the swift, and any stumble on his part and half
the blooms would be on the ground. "Don't keep me waiting while you pick them up, idiot. What's left will have to
do."

Nana was not invited to go to the cemetery since she
was, in fact, no kin to the dead. She didn't mind at all,
as the dishes could be washed and put away and dinner
started. It was strange to think of her, going cold blooded
about her work while they went through the heartbreaking
prayer for the dead. "Now," said his father, choking up to
ad lib, "we ask Thy mercy for 'precious friends hid in
death's dateless night.'"

(Papa had been a professor of English once, down at
Tulane, and then—Nana would fall into a whisper—he
somehow lost track. Of what, she didn't say. He must be
treated with veneration, all he'd suffered, and now his
eyes, what they called hysterical blindness.

His mother, that time he had been in New Orleans to
register, asked such a rude question, did his father break
down in the cemetery and weep? He had said he hadn't
noticed. She, his mother, was thin with a certainty about
her, wrapped in selfhood, his father said. Women were going downhill from good ones like Nana, who was "dieted
in grace.")

"Please note," his father said, "that the word Shake-
speare uses is *hid,* not *lost.* No one is lost to God."

Before they would leave the cemetery, they must scan

the sky for rain. Their marble bird, said to be a dove, was perched on a tombstone, its expression unconcerned, almost scornful. It was vulnerable Carrara and had to be covered in wet weather. A tattered piece of canvas was kept under the tombstone for whoever saw rain coming first.

———

The best part of the week was when their old friend Roosevelt came on Saturday afternoon. He brought a fresh supply of bourbon and Solari's order from downriver, steaks and shrimp, French bread and avocados. Roosevelt was a big man in the county, manager of some twenty-five thousand acres known as the Moon Range that had been pieced up from a string of ruined plantations. He bowed to Nana and helped her put away the groceries. Why, Miss Julie at Solari's had guessed they meant to get caviar and had put it in the order on her own.

Next, Roosevelt would bring in the heavy Talking Books for the Blind and carry them to the sacrosanct front bedroom. The door, left slightly ajar, would be closed with care. But it didn't matter, their privacy was only imagined. In the cellar an old pipe protruded which carried their voices to him. To reach the pipe and settle down to listen required zigzagging down the cellar steps so as to miss the worst snaps and creaks, then getting used to the peculiar aspect of this lower floor. A cancerous mouse ran under the water heater, its whiskers giving off dust. Old tack hung from the rafters over unkempt stacks of magazines.

Their voices from the pipe were clear, although he missed the question his father always asked and only heard the answer. "OK, I guess," Roosevelt said, "cattle and hogs anyway." He laughed. "Come down from Chicago last week, do some hunting. Ever see people afraid of snakes? These fellows, everywhere they look is a cottonmouth."

The pipe laughed, both voices. His father was to inform Roosevelt exactly when he was going to die, so it was not yet. The squeaking of the rocker was still another sign of God's mercy.

"Did they get anything?"

"Mosquitoes. Put on so much bug stuff I say, Listen. Deer can smell. Thirty, forty deer come out the bamboo every time I feed. But no indeed, Roosevelt, we sportsmen. Got to shoot them in the woods."

"Sweet princeling," Nana was jarring him awake, making him feel out of sorts. "What are you doing down here? Go wash and tell Papa supper's ready."

The voice from the pipe was the great voice of Alexander Scourby.

In the dining room for baked chicken and oyster dressing, "I have an announcement to make," said his father. "Roosevelt tells me there's a new house going up in King's Town. Being built from scratch." He paused. "This despite the fact that our historical mansions are most of them falling down. Furthermore," he frowned menacingly, "nobody knows who it is."

"Goodness gracious," said Nana. She had been smiling absently at the tablecloth, and now she stopped chewing and swallowed so that her sagging throat worked up and down. "With Margaret Maury's house full of pigeons since she died and a limb knocked out her library window."

"That's just it. General Miles's Greek Revival falling in. Who would have the gall to move into this county and start building a brand new house?"

"Think of it, who indeed? But if there's no danger it would be very educational for Dana to go and watch. Something to see, well, an experience."

"Hold on, dear Nana. He—I mean *you,* Dana—could write a paper on it, as you will be obliged to do many a time at school. Totally objective. Describe the boards, even the denomination of the nails, all the details, doors, windows, no mawkish introspection. Get it down on paper for Nana to critique."

There seemed no way to answer. His father had him blocked. If he tried to resist it would be considered impolite. And he hated to be in King's Town where people he didn't know knew him, or anyhow looked at him funny. He had kept it a secret that the barber asked him how many bottles his old man killed in a week.

He had seen them get carried away with an idea before, always to improve his chances in the world, and now to write up a house he didn't even care about. But they were in hot pursuit of the plan because even before the dishes were cleared Nana followed his father into the front bedroom, where they lowered their voices. He had to make it fast to the cellar. Their murmurings came feebly down the pipe. "It is his duty to trust our judgment . . . he must not lose his grip on reality. And then of course what happened with Maybelline." This had been the most awful example.

Maybelline. Above the sound of his pounding heart he did not try to listen any longer. Ever since the little girl died and he thought he saw her in the hall again, she was in the back of his mind. He told himself versions of that time, one sliding out of the way to be replaced by another. But now, much later, nothing was certain. Go over it once more.

She had come alone to get water, cut through the woods, it must have been scary. A tiny girl, no bigger than a mite, as Nana put it. But complete, with plaited hair, perfect hands and feet, a clean dress. At first on those visits she didn't say anything, just handed over the jug to Nana to fill at the sink. When they tried to talk to her she finally said one sentence. "I have to go home," she said. Then she was willing to talk with him little by little. "Where do you live, Maybelline?" After a long time she pointed toward the woods. "Yonder." "It's by Miss Carrie Buck's," Nana explained. "More than a mile, it must be." "I have to go home," she would say in her lilting lisp. But each time she would stay a little longer. "Wait, Maybelline. You can't go until I start you on the alphabet." And he got his old blocks out of the cupboard. "We will start with A, B, C." She was crazy about a pencil. "Don't take it home, goose, you'll lose it." He took it from her to hear the funny treble. "Give me back that pencil," she would say.

"In your relationship with colored," his father taught, "return good to those who have been so good to us." So, it was doing good for him to teach Maybelline her letters. She loved rhymes. "I had a hen / and the hen pleased me." "Go on." "I fed my hen / by yonder tree." She would bob her head and laugh.

As fall turned toward winter Nana would come into the hall. "It's getting cooler toward evening, Maybelline. Dark so early." One afternoon she went to the attic and brought down an old red coat with a hood. "Put this on so the hunters can notice you. And start now, baby, get home while you can see."

Every day she came the sun touched the red coat as it shone through the doorlights, fixing to go down over the river.

They fought over learning new rhymes. She wanted to say the same one over and over. Finally he had given in to her ways, in to pleasing her. When she wanted her way she put her tongue between her teeth and ducked her head, smiling.

Time was reckoned that winter by the arrival of the little girl in the red coat with the empty milk jug. If Maybelline didn't come by dinner she came right after. And Nana had to stop them from playing earlier and earlier as the days got short.

The rains, once they started, acted like they would never let up. The cemetery bird was covered and they used the little chapel behind the dining room for prayers. Nana assured him that Maybelline's family was getting water from their gutter. They have a gutter that carries roof water into a barrel. Many a gallon at this rate, no need to come here now.

The hall was gloomy and empty of a little girl's silliness. Nana turned on the lamps, one on the piano that glowed comfortingly. His father made him sit beside the bed and read *Great Expectations* aloud. It seemed as if night, with the relief of hugging the pillow, would never come. He was hugging it tighter and tighter, asking it spooky questions until it became his father's flabby cheek, never offered.

Every rainy morning was like every other. Then came headlights down the cemetery lane until the weak daylight showed an old black car sloshing through the mud. It stopped right under his window. Slowly a heavy person in a long apron got out and ran up under the eaves. There was Nana, back of the sweet olive, her arms full of Solari sacks. J. and M. Solari. After they hugged each other Nana came out in the rain, pushing the other toward the car, stuffing the sacks in after her. The motor started and an arm flew out the window, pointing to the sky where clouds still scudded up from the Gulf. "Heaven," the fat person yelled, and Nana, nodding, watched the car back up in the mud and turn around.

He ran to the kitchen in his bare feet. The screen door opened and Nana came back in, beads of rain on her faded hair. "It was Maybelline's grandmother," she said, "called last night for funeral finery and we had a baked ham. The angels have swooped her to heaven."

At his father's door the knock was not answered. He went in anyway, to the scent of ammonia and juniper berries. "'Fear no more the heat o' the sun / Nor the furious winter's rages.'"

Knowing and not knowing, he ran back to the hall. The lamp on the piano lighted the red flannel lining of the cutlery box and suddenly she was back. Her silliness made him dizzy, and he began to laugh and cry and laugh some more until they made him swallow a pill and go to sleep.

It was the form grief took. That was his mother over long-distance telephone putting in her two cents' worth. The only child he knew. And his father said he paid her and everybody else, so he would pay the psychiatrist to diagnose faulty perception, patient sight unseen. "Handy later on when we go jingoistic again."

Nana was reasonable. "You mustn't see things that are not there. Our little friend is in heaven, not the hall." Had he said she was in the hall? "If you want to remember her, fine. The happy times you had when she came for water. We have to stick to the truth."

Roosevelt began bringing him new books from up in Natchez. Nana went on walks in the woods to teach him the names of trees and the nesting patterns of birds. Best of all, Maybelline was added to the cemetery supplications as soon as the rains stopped.

"Is she with Jesus?"

"Of course," his father admitted crossly. "Jesus said: 'Where I am, there ye may be also.'"

Certainty flooded the cemetery. She was stored up for later on.

———

Haircut Saturday came, but instead Roosevelt was to drive him to see the new house. That and the haircut might be too much for one day, they thought. His notebook had lines so that he could jot down this, that, and the other, no need for sentences yet, just get an idea, a kind of inventory.

Driving out of the sunken cut to the highway, then on into King's Town, everything looked different. The collapsing mansions of King and Queen Street seemed somehow withdrawn. Even the Catholic church looked askance at the Moon Range's pickup. It was his role of spy, that was it, wrong but a necessary step on the way to New Orleans and Holy Name.

He could see himself at Holy Name, addressing a covey of girls. When he'd been there with his mother he had picked out two in the hall when classes were changing. One with dark, fine hair, short, Martha, he decided, and the other one with pop eyes, blue, dangerous looking. He could call a few of them together, including those two. They would listen to what he had to say, with him making it up as he went along. He could hear his tone, like his father's, stern and terribly sad. "That's all for now," he would say, turn his back and forget every one of them.

The new house was on Confederate Street. As they drove up to the curb, Roosevelt so casual and homey, he was surprised by the strong smell of new lumber. Poised with the notebook, what could he write about the carpenters, all dressed in white, hammering away. Everybody knew that carpenters hammered, so put "all dressed in white." One thing stood out as curious. The cemetery bird was perched on the roof, its marble feathers unruffled. "What is that bird doing here?"

Roosevelt squinted up. "Tar paper and Sheetrock," he said. "Sure look to be a bird."

The dove disappeared into its explanation, but its spirit lagged an instant, aloof and unrepentant.   ✧

BERRY MORGAN was born in 1919 in Port Gibson, Mississippi. She teaches at the Catholic University of America and writes from her home in West Virginia. Ms. Morgan has had a long career of publishing in *The New Yorker* and elsewhere.

SPIRIT VOICES

J turned twenty-seven
on a quiet Saturday in April, shortly after the birth of our
second child. The day was dull and ominous: it had been
raining off and on since I woke, and I spent most of the
morning working on our taxes. My birthday gifts had been
practical—socks, underwear, shirts in a style that made me
feel that I wasn't really young anymore. When I went out
for a drive in the late afternoon, the light drizzle began to
turn to sleet, and the houses, the telephone poles, the street
signs, became sharp-edged and spectral against the gray
sky. Dark birds lifted out of the bare trees as I passed.

I had only meant to go to the drugstore, but as I turned
onto the quiet main street, I thought I saw my brother-
in-law's wife, Rhonda, the one my wife's family hated,
driving alone in a long white car. Though I knew it was
foolish, I couldn't help but follow.

We'd known for a week or so that she was back, but I
hadn't seen her. In the dark weather, I couldn't even be
certain it *was* her—I only caught a glimpse of the face, the
pale skin and short black hair. I drifted behind the car as it
headed out toward the edge of town.

The town we live in is small by most standards, little
more than a cluster of trees and buildings in the middle of

the prairie—a main street the teenagers drive up and down at night, with a few storefronts in the center, the town wisping away at both ends into gas stations, motels, then open road. The car was going under the viaduct, to the west side, where I knew Rhonda was staying.

Rhonda lived in a low-income tract called Sioux Villa, and most of the residents there were pretty bad off—destitute elderly, single mothers, Indians, alcoholics. If there was a murder in St. Bonaventure, it usually happened in Sioux Villa. The apartments were in rows of six, so that the place looked like the old one-story stucco motel my family had owned until I was seven, when my father bought the more elegant Bonaventure Motor Lodge.

I didn't know which apartment Rhonda lived in, so I cruised in and out of the rows until I saw that white car parked in front of one of the unnumbered doorways.

I stopped the car. That was all—I didn't have any plan in mind. I idled the car outside, listening to the rain, to the rhythmic wing-beating of the windshield wipers. The defroster was on high, and the car smelled heavy with it.

Then I pulled the hood up on my jacket and opened the car door, but I left the engine running. I thought, why not be a good person? I thought, why not go ring her bell, and tell her welcome back. I imagined myself saying: "If there's anything you need, give us a call," though I knew Susan, my wife, wouldn't want anything to do with her. Susan would probably hang up on her if she called.

I hesitated there on her stoop, thinking of this. I remembered Susan telling me: "If I see her, I have half a mind to kick her ass. Seriously." The rain trickled from my hood, and I wiped the droplets from my glasses, leaving a blurry film before my eyes. Maybe this wasn't even her place.

I opened the screen door and pressed my face close to the little diamond-shaped window in the inside door. I cupped my hand over my eyes and peered in. The window was fogged over: droplets of condensation ran down the steamy glass, leaving little bars through which I could spot an old Naugahyde couch, a crumpled bag of potato chips lying on it. Then, just at the edge of my vision, I spotted an arm. I leaned closer, and the rest of her tilted into view: she was standing at the mouth of a dark hallway, with her back to me. I saw that she was shirtless, and as I watched, she pushed her jeans down to her ankles and stepped out of them. She was a small woman, yet her body was hard-looking, almost muscular; different, somehow, from the shapes of women I was used to seeing around St. B. She stood there in her underwear and stocking feet for a moment, looking down at something I couldn't see. Then her shoulders tightened, and her arms contorted behind her back as she unhooked her bra. My own breath was fogging up the outside glass, and as I passed my hand through the condensation she turned, startled. She crossed her arms over her bare breasts: she'd seen my face at the window, I thought, and my heart leapt. What was I doing? Peeping in—a person could get arrested for that. I let the screen door slam and backed away quickly, hurrying toward my idling car: how could I explain myself to Rhonda now, or worse, what would Susan say if she found out? My body felt luminous, visible.

I put the car in reverse, and my wheels spun in the wet gravel. I spun out of the row of houses, and as I turned the corner, I caught a glimpse of her as she stumbled to the door. I stepped on the gas, and as I roared away, I could see her standing on the doorstep in only a towel, her hands tented over her head to shield herself from the rain. I imagined I heard her shouting something after me.

———

Afterward, when I thought of what I'd done, I felt actually trembly with embarrassment and confusion. What if she'd recognized the car? What if she'd seen me? I'd never really known Rhonda that well, not enough to think of her as a friend, anyway. I'd talked to her a few times at family gatherings, and we'd seemed to hit it off. There was a kind of cynical edge in what she said, and I secretly relished her dry comments about our in-laws, the loose, almost bored posture as she sat, listening to them talk. I remembered the Thanksgiving afternoon when she sipped casually from a pint bottle of peach schnapps after dinner, reclining in the living room, watching sports while the rest of the women washed dishes. I was the one who sat next to her. But the vague camaraderie between us was not enough to justify my behavior. It might even give Rhonda the idea that I was after her, a married man eager to prey on a "fallen woman."

It had been six months since Rhonda left my wife's brother, Kent, and their two-year-old daughter. She'd run off with a Puerto Rican, so people said. Rhonda and Kent had been living in Virginia at the time. Kent had just been discharged from the Navy, where he'd learned a trade—some kind of mechanics, I gathered—and he was looking for a job when she went off. My mother-in-law claimed the Puerto Rican was both a pimp and a dope dealer, and had gotten Rhonda hooked on something. In any case, Kent came home to Nebraska with his little girl, and I gave him a job at the motel I run—the motel I inherited from my father. My mother-in-law cared for the child while he was at work.

Kent got a few letters from Rhonda, but he didn't let anyone know what they said. And then, after several months, Rhonda appeared in St. Bonaventure. My mother-in-law imagined that the man had beat her up and dumped her somewhere along their "journey of sin," a journey she'd followed through the postmarks on the letters—Atlantic City, Philadelphia, Baltimore. She talked of these cities as if they were distant constellations.

Ever since Rhonda returned, my mother-in-law had been imagining that she wanted Kent back. "He'd have to be out of his mind," she murmured when Kent was out of the room. But I guess I wasn't so sure.

It wasn't that I approved of what Rhonda had done, of course. But I wasn't sure that I blamed her, either. I wanted to know her side of the story.

When I got home, my sister Joan was there. She had come to cook us dinner. We had planned to go out dancing for my birthday that night, but by the afternoon we decided to postpone until some other time. The baby was colicky, and our two-year-old, Joshua, hadn't taken well to his change in status. Recently, he'd begun to wake up in the middle of the night, too, calling for us jealously. So Joan said she was going to come over and fix us a steak.

My sister was six years older than me. My mother had had two miscarriages in between us, and perhaps that had hardened Joan to the idea of siblings. In any case, we'd never been close as children, not, in fact, until after our parents had passed away and Joan had divorced. There wasn't any real reason for her to stay in St. Bonaventure besides me, I guess.

Joan looked at me shrewdly when I came in. She often seemed to loom over people, though she wasn't exactly tall—just, as she put it, big-boned. "Where were you?" she said. "I've been here for nearly an hour."

"I was driving," I told her, and she nodded. She was big on the notion of "private time." Everyone in our family had been, in individual ways, a bit of a loner. Still, I couldn't picture her following someone for no reason, or peeping into their home.

"Where's Susan?" I said, and she looked back to the green pepper she was dissecting.

"She's in the bedroom with the baby. The J-monster is in there, too." She had recently started to be a little antagonistic toward Joshua. I could tell she thought he was spoiled, but it still surprised me. She'd always seemed so delighted by him before. Not too long ago, she'd told me that she was glad she never had any children of her own. I hoped she wouldn't keep calling Joshua the J-monster.

"Any major disasters while I was out?" I asked.

"Just the usual," she said. "Tell Susan dinner will be ready soon."

Susan was sitting on our bed, nursing Molly and reading a book to Joshua. He huddled into the crook of her arm, listening grimly. I sat down beside her, with Joshua between us, and I slipped my arm around her waist, encompassing all of them.

"'They passed the restless ocean,'" Susan read, "'combing out her hair.'" She winked at me. "What took you so long?" she said.

"Oh, I got lost," I said. "It's the perfect day for the end of my youth." I put my hand to my brow melodramatically.

"Come on," she said. "You're not allowed to brood until you turn thirty."

"I'm advanced," I said, and Joshua pushed against us impatiently. "Read," he said. "Read." And so Susan continued, and I looked down at Molly. She was nursing intensely, her eyes closed, her brow furrowed. Susan hadn't breast-fed Joshua, and it was still strange to see her breasts, with their new roundness, almost opaque so I could just barely see her veins deep beneath her skin. She had always been hearty and athletic-looking, and the leftover softness of pregnancy made her seem almost exotic. We hadn't made love since the baby was born, and I hadn't pressed her, yet. But sometimes, when her nipple slipped out of the baby's mouth, erect and red, I would feel a twinge of urgency. And then, almost involuntarily, I thought of Rhonda, the flash of the brown aureoles of her breasts before her pale arms covered them. I cleared my throat.

"Joan says supper's almost ready," I said, and Susan nodded.

———

At supper, Joan insisted on a chorus of "Happy Birthday," and I sat there, listening to their low, female voices intertwining, echoing hollowly. Joshua watched with amazed horror. Afterward, Joan went right into one of her heavy conversations. There were several recurring themes when Joan visited—her ex-husband, and what had happened to her marriage; her dislike for St. Bonaventure; lack of suitable male companionship, etc. Tonight, she told us that her boss, a married man, wanted to have an affair with her.

"The worst part of it," she said, "is that we're friends, sort of. At least, I have to work closely with him every day. It's not like I can just say 'screw you' and forget about it. I can see what it is. His wife is this matronly country-club type, and he's got what? Three or four kids. And I think it's something that all married people go through at some point. Especially men."

"Plus you're pretty," my wife said. "And vulnerable."

"What do you mean, 'especially men,'" I said.

"Oh, shut up," Joan told me. "Not *you*." Joshua got up from the table, and I warned him that the baby was sleeping. He turned his back to me, bitterly, and sat down among his toys. "Anyway," Joan said. "The truth is, in a lot of ways, I'm really attracted to him, and I would do it, I would. But look at me. I've been divorced for almost as long as I was married now, and I've passed the point in my life when I could allow that sort of thing to happen to me. I mean, here I am in this tiny town, with his wife and children living right here, and him involved in all these domestic things. I wouldn't be able to call him if I wanted. We'd have to sneak around, quickies on abandoned roads, that sort of thing. I'm sure that's just the kind of adventure he'd love. But me? I'd end up like what's-her-name. Your brother's wife. Rhonda. Wandering around St. Bonaventure like a spook."

"Don't do it," my wife said. "You deserve better. You really do."

"Yeah," Joan said. "I know I do." She cut her steak carefully, glancing down to where Joshua was driving a toy truck against her foot. She made a face. "So what's with the whole Rhonda thing, anyway? Anything new?"

"Not that I know of," Susan said. She looked over at me, and it sent a sudden prickle across my neck. "It's still in progress, as far as I know," she said. She shot me another quick look, one that was meant to convey sympathy for Joan.

"Poor Joan," Susan would say later, when we were up with the baby in the middle of the night. "I wish there was something we could do for her." She went on to remark on how sweet and smart and good-looking Joan was. "Why doesn't someone wonderful come along for her," she asked, and I murmured, "I don't know." But the truth was, I thought, even if a wonderful man came along, he wouldn't be good enough. At least Rhonda had made a choice. Joan acted like she could go through life, making excuses but never *doing* anything, as if there were an infinity of possibilities to choose from. Sooner or later she was going to find those possibilities were disappearing, one by one. But I wouldn't tell Susan this, because generalities annoyed her. "What possibilities?" she'd ask. "Disappeared how?" and I wouldn't be able to explain.

———

Saturdays were my only day off, and in the morning I was back to work at the motel. I tried to put all the thoughts of the previous day—of Rhonda, and my sister, and disappearing possibilities—out of my mind. To a certain extent, I guess, I was feeling a little guilty. I kept imagining that Rhonda had recognized me, and I pictured her eventually getting back together with Kent, telling him. I tried to think of what I would say to Susan. I knew how she would interpret it: I secretly had the hots for Rhonda, she'd say. I was getting restless. That's what she would think, no matter how carefully I explained myself.

Susan honestly hated Rhonda. "She's beneath contempt," she'd always say. "How could a mother leave her child like that, for any reason?" In a way, I suppose, I was surprised at the hard edge in her voice, just as I was surprised at how easily she'd settled into being a mother. She had once been pretty wild herself, and I thought she'd have more sympathy.

When we first met, Susan had seemed so dangerous to me: she hung around with older men, who gave her rides on their motorcycles and in their jacked-up cars, and she was a drinker. I guess it was what I needed at the time. My mother had just died, and my father had just had the first in the series of strokes that would eventually kill him. He once told me that the best thing he'd ever done was to be there for his parents when they were old—his brothers were never around—and that stuck with me. I'd come home from college to help with the motel, and Susan would come over late and talk me into turning on the "No Vacancy" light before we'd filled. She'd get me to do things I never would have done without her. I still thought fondly of how we'd stayed up all night, how she and her tough girlfriends taught me how to bounce a quarter into a glass of beer, or the time she'd tricked me into trying marijuana by feeding it to me in a cake. We used to drive a hundred miles just to check into small-town motels, pretending we were having an illicit affair. Once, an old woman had refused to give us a room because we didn't have the same last name. "I don't believe in it," she told us darkly.

When I walked into the office of the motel, Kent was asleep, slumped in the swivel chair behind the desk. He worked the night shift, from ten until seven, and usually the motel was as full as it was going to get by the time he started. He didn't have to deal much with customers at all, and I figured he would be good at taking care of the type of problems that sometimes arise late at night. He was a big man, with thick, dark eyebrows and a kind of steely, mean-looking face. He was a nice enough person, actually, though I remembered being afraid of him when we first met.

Of course, my father wouldn't have liked to see him there, unshaven, a full ashtray on the desk, his heavy head tucked against his shoulder. My parents had always run the place themselves. We'd lived in the little three-bed-room apartment connected to the office, and my mother or father had registered every guest. There was a buzzer at the front that brought them, no matter what the hour, out of bed.

I'd hired out. The little apartment behind the office had been converted into storage. Still, I was there six days a week, ten hours a day. I hadn't abandoned the place.

I rang the bell, and Kent stirred a little, his brow furrowing. "Fuck," he murmured. Then he opened his eyes, glowering up at whoever had disturbed him.

I frowned. "Rise and shine," I said. "Shift's over."

"Oh," he said, and his look softened. "Robert. Hey, happy birthday, man."

"Thanks," I said. "You know . . . you really have to be careful about your language around the guests."

"Yeah," he said, and looked down. "I know it. Sorry about that." He glanced around sheepishly, as if there might be someone else in the room, and his look reminded me that he'd had a rough time of it lately. I didn't want to be another problem in his life.

"It's no big deal," I said. "Any major disasters last night?"

"Nada," he said. "All quiet. Did you and Sue go out?"

I shrugged. "In a few weeks, maybe. Joan came over and

fixed us a nice dinner." I shrugged again, as if I had to make excuses, to apologize. "It was all right," I said.

Kent nodded, and his voice dropped a little, the way men's voices do when they exchange something that passes for personal. I'd never been exactly sure what it meant. "Yeah, well, I know how it is, man." He smiled, pursing his lips. "I guess maybe I'm lucky to be a bachelor again."

"Yes, well," I said. I wished that I could ask him what was going on between him and Rhonda. He surely must have known she was in town. Had he seen her? Talked to her? "So how are things going with you?" I said. "You're getting along OK?"

"Oh, fine." Now it was Kent's turn to shrug. "Brittany's running Mom ragged. You know how Mom can get to complaining. But she loves it, you can tell." He sighed, and stood up. His hair was flattened on one side, stiff as paper. I watched as he tried to neaten the clutter on the desk, piling the scattered papers together. "I guess you heard that Rhonda's back in town," he said at last.

"Yeah," I said.

"Yeah," he said. "Fucking everybody's heard." He stared into my eyes, and I tried to keep my face noncommittal, but I could feel my expression wavering, the muscles moving beneath the skin. Finally he looked away and picked up his ashtray, dumping it into the wastebasket. "I don't know, man," he said. "I just don't know."

———

The motel, the Bonaventure Motor Lodge, was not the most profitable business around. The town was in a valley and couldn't be seen by cars passing on the interstate. All they could see were the mesas and treeless hills, the empty pastureland that surrounded us, and despite the cheerful signs that promised food, gas, lodging, most of them just kept on going. Still, there were always a few forced to straggle in come nightfall, enough to keep us in business.

I liked to watch them in the mornings, as they loaded up their vehicles and went on their various ways. This time of year, there weren't too many vacationers. They were mostly, I imagined, off on more desperate pursuits: nomadic men and women, fugitives, lovers, addled old folks, young families on their way to new jobs, working men fleeing their dying cities, or parts of families, single mothers and fathers, escaping some domestic situation. There was something heroic about these people, I thought. I would walk down the row, glancing at the license plates, peeking in the windows of the cars. You could tell a lot about people from what they left in the back seats of their cars: toys, books, empty beer cans, little barking dogs with their toenails painted bright red. Once I saw a semi-automatic, tossed as if casually on a blanket in the back; another time, a limbless mannequin gazed blankly at me when I peered into a hatchback. For a minute, I thought it was a body. Sometimes, when I was sure no one was looking, I would trace my name or my initials in the dusty film on the back of a car. Sometimes, I would be out there when a guest came out the door, and I'd talk to them for a bit—ask them if they slept comfortably, inquire casually as to where they were headed. Mostly, people didn't have much to say. To them, I was just another provincial busybody, another obstacle in their path.

———

In the afternoon, after all the keys had been turned in, and while the maids were cleaning out the rooms, my sister stopped by for lunch. She was working at the courthouse, in the County Attorney's office, and she hadn't been getting along with her co-workers—she didn't want to spend her lunch period with them. They were all secretary types, dumb as dirt, she said. Besides, she suspected they had been gossiping about her and Mr. Trencher, her boss.

She'd brought a bucket of chicken from a local fast-food place, and we ate in the apartment in back of the office, in the old kitchen. The table we'd had when we were kids was still there, though the kitchen itself was cluttered with fresh towels and boxes of toilet paper and complimentary soap. "Don't you find it a little creepy, eating back here," Joan said as she spread out the plastic silverware and plates and opened the Styrofoam containers of mashed potatoes and gravy. "I think of all the hours Mother spent in this kitchen, and now look at it. It would kill her to see."

"I think it's sort of comforting, actually," I said. "Nostalgic."

"You would," she said. She peeled the crisp skin off her chicken and set it on my plate. "Trencher's been moon-eyed all morning," she said. "It's really driving me crazy."

"Tell him to cut it out," I said. "Give him a karate chop."

She grimaced. "Well," she said. "It's not like he's chasing me around the desk or something. That's the trouble. It's this very subtle thing—little looks, and this weird tension in the air. So if I tell him to cut it out, he can act like I'm just paranoid. He'll say I'm reading things into it."

I nodded slowly, scoping my mind for good advice. I didn't know what she expected me to say. I didn't understand this Mr. Trencher any more than I understood Rhonda, or Joan herself, whose unfaithful ex-husband used to call late at night, used to drive hundreds of miles to camp out on her door. Why did she seem to draw this type of man? I had never been a person who could follow that kind of love, with its hidden agendas and uncertainty, its mazes of fear and desire. I hadn't been in love very many times. As far as I knew, my wife was the only woman who'd ever been in love with me. What did I know about any of it? "You could quit," I suggested hesitantly.

"Why should I have to quit," she said sharply. I shrugged: she was right, I hadn't been thinking. "I didn't do anything wrong. If anything, I should file harassment charges," she said.

I nodded. "You could." But then she just pursed her

lips. It seemed a distant possibility; and as we looked at one another, I had the strange feeling that she wasn't completely unhappy with the situation. We ate for a moment in silence.

I was trying to think of some other subject to bring up when the front-desk buzzer rang. I scooted my chair back, and Joan stood up as I did.

"I've got to get going anyway," Joan said. "I've got some errands to run."

But when we walked out to the office, both of us stopped cold. Rhonda was standing at the desk, and when she saw Joan, her eyes narrowed. She glanced from Joan to me, holding herself stiffly, formally, like a messenger. She was wearing one of those coats that looked like it was made out of red vinyl, the kind a rock singer might wear, with big shoulder pads. But her face looked tired and drawn. She stared at me, and I felt myself blushing, for a moment imagining she had come to accuse me of spying on her.

"I wanted to leave this for Kent," she said, and held out an envelope. She set it on the desk, on top of the guest register. "I heard he was working here."

"He's not here now," I said, and she brushed her eyes over me, a quick once-over. She kept her face expressionless.

"I know," she said. "Could you just see that Kent gets it?"

"Sure," I said, and she turned, without looking at me again, and went out the door. I was almost as surprised by the abruptness of her exit as I had been to see her standing there. I guess I had imagined some little conversation between us, some slight acknowledgment. I watched her car pull through the motel's cul-de-sac and back onto the street.

"Well, well," Joan said. She breathed, a sigh that seemed somewhere between puzzled and gratified. "This should be interesting. I can hardly wait for Susan to hear about this." She looked at me sidelong and I watched her gently lift the envelope. For a moment, I thought she was going to open it, and it sent an odd, possessive jolt through me. I wanted to snatch it from her. But she just examined it, front and back: blank. Then she put it down. "I'll drop by the house after work," she said.

———

Susan didn't say much at first. Miraculously, both babies were asleep, and she was stretched out on the couch, watching music videos. I sat down and she slid her feet onto my lap. "So you didn't open this letter, I suppose," she said at last.

"Of course not," I said.

"Hmmmm," she said. I ran my thumb along the sole of her bare foot, reproachfully, and she shifted, stretching her leg muscles. "I'd like to know what that bitch is telling him." She leaned her head back, looking at me thoughtfully.

"You could ask Kent," I said.

"Yeah, right," she said. "If my mom hasn't gotten it out of him, then no one will." She eyed me for a minute, and when my finger grazed the underside of her foot again, she moved her feet from my lap and tucked them beneath her. "He still loves her, I suppose," she said. "*Thinks* he loves her."

"Could be," I agreed. But I wasn't sure what the difference was, between loving someone and thinking you do. It made me uncomfortable, puzzling over it, because it suggested layers of reality—what you thought was solid suddenly gave way, like a secret panel in a haunted house. "Maybe she thinks she loves him, too," I said.

"Oh, I'm sure," Susan said. She squinted, as if trying to see something far in the distance. "I'm sure that's the line she's feeding him, among others. 'Kent, I made a little mistake,'" she mimicked, in a soft, breathy voice—nothing like Rhonda's, I thought. Susan pouted her lips. "'I'm so-o sorry,'" she purred.

"Well . . . ," I said hesitantly. "Maybe she did make a mistake." I shrugged, and she peered at me, the corners of her mouth moving vaguely, a Mona Lisa smile.

"That's not a mistake," she said at last. "A mistake is when your account is overdrawn a few bucks at the bank. It isn't a mistake when you leave your husband and baby daughter to run off with some pimp." Her expression shifted again, but I couldn't guess what she was thinking. "If I were to do something like that, is that what you'd call it? A mistake?"

"I'd take you back," I said.

"No you wouldn't," she said. "You may think you would, but I know you. You wouldn't." I couldn't help but flinch a little, pinned by that look. What did she see in me, or think she saw? She shook her head. "Besides," she said. "I wouldn't go back if you'd have me. I couldn't respect you." We stared at each other, and I couldn't think of what to say next. The baby monitor crackled in the silence, humming with transistor noise. We waited. I saw her straighten, tensing like an animal seen briefly in a clearing, before it bolts. "Oh, no," she whispered, and Molly's voice, that high, eerie mechanical cry that infants have, began to unravel, soft at first, but gaining force.

When Joan showed up a while later, I was walking the baby, trying to quiet her. Susan and Joan sat down at the kitchen table, and I could hear Susan going on in the same vein. "I've told Kent what my opinion is," she was saying. I didn't concentrate on the rest. The baby kept wailing, her cries shuddering in my ears. The radio was turned up, playing static in hopes that the white noise might calm her, as it sometimes did. But it was having the opposite effect on me: the radio and the crying baby and the bitter voices of the women in the next room layered over me, like hot, stale air, and when I looked into the kitchen, I was surprised by the shudder of disgust that passed through me. I stared at them from the threshold, and I couldn't help but think how primitive they seemed, like pictures of Russian peasant women I'd seen in books, with their hard, judgmental mouths and their drab clothes. At that moment, they seemed to represent everything that was small and compromised and unlovely about my life. I thought about the time I'd gotten into Joan's car and found the radio tuned to a Muzak station; I thought about the scuffed terrycloth house slippers my wife had taken to wearing, even in the middle of the day. They should want to run off with dark-skinned lovers, I thought, they should want to do crazy drugs and wander through strange cities after midnight. I rocked Molly insistently, shushing her without much gentleness in my voice.

"Has your mother heard about it?" Joan was saying. Susan was at the refrigerator, and I watched as she took out a single beer and poured it into two glasses. I thought sadly of those nights before we were married, walking her home after we'd been out drinking, Susan leaning against me, her lips pressed close to my ear. All that stuff, I thought, was behind us; now she couldn't even manage to drink a whole beer by herself.

"I pray to God she doesn't," Susan said. She offered Joan the glass of beer, and I watched them both take little sips. "She's on twenty-four-hour watch as it is."

"I'm sure," Joan said. She smiled—grotesquely, I thought, enjoying herself. "But don't you think Rhonda's going to eventually want to see the baby?"

"Not if Mom can help it."

"That's ridiculous," I said, and they both looked up. Molly had quieted a bit, and maybe they hadn't noticed me listening. "They can't keep her from seeing her own child," I said, and the pulse of annoyance I felt toward them crept into my voice. "I mean, legally, doesn't she have visitation rights or something?"

They both eyed me. Susan made a wry face, and the way

she tilted her head made me realize she needed a haircut. It constantly looked like it needed to be combed, and the word *unbecoming* came suddenly into my mind. "She'd need a damn good lawyer," Susan said. "And if you think she's going to get past Mom without a fight, you don't know my mother." She let her gaze linger over me for a moment, and I frowned. "He's been Rhonda's biggest fan lately," she told Joan.

"Oh, I know," Joan said. "You should have seen them making goo-goo eyes at each other at the motel." It was supposed to be a joke, but I felt my face getting warm. I wasn't in the mood for Joan's humor. "Little do we know," Joan said. "He's actually Rhonda's secret sex slave."

"Shut up, Joan," I said. "That's all you think about, isn't it? Why don't you just sleep with Trencher and get it over with." I hesitated, a little taken aback by my own meanness, but before Joan could say anything, Molly started to shriek again, and the sound made my shoulders go rigid, made my whole body hum with irritation. "Jesus Christ!" I snapped at Susan. "Can you please take this brat off my hands—she wants to nurse." I thrust the baby toward her, and her cries stopped abruptly; her tiny eyes widened in terror or accusation. Then her mouth contorted and she screamed again.

"What's wrong with you? Are you crazy?" Glaring, she took the baby and cradled her gently, sheltering her from me.

"How do you expect me to get her to sleep with you two in here harping away like a couple of old biddies?" I said. Susan lifted her blouse roughly, and the baby affixed herself desperately to the breast, as if she'd been held against her will and starved by some torturer. "Oh, it makes me sick," I said. "My whole life is nothing but work and screaming kids and listening to you two gossip and complain. I'm so bored and tired of this same old thing that I could just jump out a window."

"Why don't you then," Susan said. "You're the one that complains all the time! All you do is sit around like a lump and brood. And now you can't even stand to take a few minutes to comfort your own sick baby. If you're so bored why don't you leave? Maybe you could hook up with your precious Rhonda. I'm sure she'd show you a great time."

"Maybe I will," I said.

"Good," Susan said. She narrowed her eyes at me, then lifted her glass and drained the beer defiantly. "There's the door."

I hesitated for a moment, opening my mouth with no words—no quick retorts or parting shots. I just stared at them, shaking my head. "I'm leaving," I said. Then I turned and walked out, slamming the door.

———

It was a cool night, full of those heavy, earthy-smelling spring shadows, and by the time I was in the car my heart was shriveling. It wasn't an anger I'd be able to hang onto very long, and I knew in a few hours I'd be turning various apologies over in my mind. At least, I thought, I'd go out to a bar; then I'd walk down to the motel and spend the night there.

I drove slowly down our street, through the tunnel of newly budding trees, the rows of my neighbors' houses with their basketball hoops above the garage doors or their toy-scattered lawns, curling down into the valley, toward Euclid Avenue. It was about nine o'clock; the movie had let out, and the high-school kids were cruising, just as I had done at their age, idling restlessly at the three stop-lights, roaring from one end of town to the other and back, honking as they passed their friends. I thought of the worn path a zoo animal makes around the circumference of its cage. They'd get out of St. Bonaventure soon, they'd graduate and never come back. That's what they were thinking.

I pulled onto Euclid, maybe the only grown-up on the

street, merging with them, pacing the twelve blocks or so between eastern and western city limits. A car full of heavily made-up teenage girls slowed, and they stretched to peer at me. I could see their mouths laughing and chattering as they passed. We had been trying to keep the kids from using the motel lot as a place to make a U-turn, but I watched them come to the end of the street and spin through the cul-de-sac at the Motor Lodge, riding the big speed bumps we'd put in as if they were some carnival ride. I could see from a distance that the "No Vacancy" light was on. But when I drove through, making my own U-turn, I counted only six cars in the lot. The office was dark, and the thought of Kent in there, fast asleep, brought back a wave of that old irritation.

As I parked the car I clenched my fists, imagining Kent huddled up in the back, eyes closed tight, breathing through his nose. I thought of the money he'd lost me; not much, probably, but it added up, it meshed with all the other worries on my mind. I was never going to get anywhere, I thought.

It was silent when I opened the door. My keys chimed against one another, dangling in the lock. "Kent?" I said sternly. I flipped the lights on and the fluorescent bulbs slowly flickered to life. Kent's dirty ashtray was on the desk, and papers were scattered everywhere. I glanced outside, thinking maybe some emergency had taken him away, but my mother-in-law's pickup, the one she let Kent drive, was still out there in the space marked "Manager."

"Kent," I called again, less certainly, and I stepped cautiously toward the dark rooms. For a moment I thought I could hear music coming from back there—vague, distant sounds, like marimba tones, bamboo wind chimes brushing one another. I used to check out this book at the library from time to time, *Omens and Superstitions of the World,* and I remembered reading that if you imagine you hear music, then you are in the presence of benevolent spirits.

It's an American Indian belief. But the music didn't sound benevolent: it seemed sad; something has been lost, I thought, and it made me shiver. The sound seemed to drift off into the distance, just barely at the edge of my hearing. Then it was gone.

"Kent," I whispered. I stood there, not really wanting to move into the shadows, imagining terrible things: Kent lying on the floor back there, with a gun still gripped in his fist, or his body swinging slowly over a tipped chair. "Hello? Is someone there?" I called. And then I noticed, lying there on the desk, the cash box—just sitting out, for all to see. I picked it up quickly and opened it. Of course it was empty, except for a few credit-card vouchers and a page of motel stationery, with Kent's handwriting on it.

"Dear Robert," I read, beneath the motel letterhead. "I know what I am doing is wrong. But part of it can count towards this week's wages I guess. I hope you will consider the rest a loan. I will pay you back as soon as I can. I am going to get back with Rhon. We will get Brittany after Mom is asleep. And go somewhere, I'm not sure. Please tell Mom that I will send for our stuff when we are settled. And tell her and Susan I am sorry and love to them. But this is the only way, it seems, because nothing can work under so much pressure and everyone's mind made up, etc. I swear I'll pay back every cent to you." It was signed "Kent Barnhart."

I didn't know how much they'd taken; there may have been almost five hundred dollars there. I'd planned to go to the bank and deposit it in the morning. But I knew this much: I couldn't really afford to lose it. I stood there at the window, the sound of my pulse beating in my ears. I stared out at the parking lot—six lousy cars. But someone would have to be there to check them out in the morning. Then, as I gazed out at the line of doorways, the familiar shape of the building, and the walk, I recognized the car at the end of the row. It was Rhonda's old white Buick.

I knew they must be in there at that very moment, in the room just in front of her car—B19, the one with the king-size bed. My muscles tightened, and for a moment I pressed my hands to the window, as if I were locked inside. I wasn't, of course; I could march down there myself and open the door with my master key, throw it open wide and demand my money back. That's what Susan would do, I thought. And if it were Joan, she'd have already been on the phone to the cops. But I was just sitting there, listening to the ticks and hums of the empty office, waiting. Coward, I thought.

I pulled my keys out of the lock and went out, moving like a burglar across my own property, hanging close to the wall. I tried to goad myself, picturing them making love on a nest of my money, picturing them mocking me. My insides felt wavery, like something seen through thick, imperfect glass, and I pinched the key tightly between my fingers. By the time I got to the door, that wavering feeling seemed to be spreading, extending beyond my body like an aura. I saw myself fit the key into the lock, sliding the metal teeth silently into the slot, and I felt my hand turning the knob. But I didn't push the door open. I hesitated there, the knob cool and smooth against my skin, and I drew my face closer to the door. I could hear voices. I inched the door open, just a crack. They were whispering, and though I held my breath, I couldn't make out the words—only gentle, sad voices, and when I pushed the door open a bit further I could see them, reflected in the dresser mirror, sitting there on the bed, their heads almost touching, holding hands. I don't know how long I stood there, staring at their reflection, but they didn't look up. I felt as if something large and dark was hovering over me, opening its wings. After a time I edged back. I let the door pull quietly closed. Then I went back to my car and drove away.

For a long time afterward, I felt ashamed of myself;

there was something unmanly, there was some weakness, I guess, in letting someone rob you and just letting them go. I never told Susan about it. When my mother-in-law called early the next morning, I acted as shocked as the rest of them.

By the time I'd gone back to the motel that night, they'd left. I'd just driven out a little beyond the edge of town and parked there by the side of the road, like Susan and I used to do. Euclid turned into Highway 30 just outside of town, and Highway 30 fed into the interstate which stretched either way across the country, toward both coasts. Even as I drove past the city limits, the big chamber of commerce welcome sign, and the glow of the all-night gas station, I knew that I was not the type of person who could ever run off, except to a life of loneliness and sorrow. My fate was already mapped out—smooth, straight lines of married and familial love—and I could see everything clearly: in a few days or weeks Susan and I would make love again, the first time in a long while, and everything would fall back in place, all would be well. Joan and Mr. Trencher would continue that slow, strange dance they'd been engaged in, and I'd keep going to work, and the children would grow, and in a hundred years there wouldn't be a trace of any of us. Maybe Rhonda and Kent would end up back in town, too, eventually, but I couldn't be certain about them. What did I know about that kind of love, that kind of life? ❧

DAN CHAON's stories have appeared in *Story, Triquarterly, Crazyhorse, Indiana Review,* and other magazines. He is currently finishing a collection of stories. Mr. Chaon lives in Cleveland with his wife, the writer Sheila Schwartz, and two sons.

URSULA K. LE GUIN

CLIMBING TO THE MOON

*L*ittle Aby will help her build the fire, running down from the dunes, his curly head like a thistle-down puff against the long gold light in the west. "Let's get the fire laid before it gets dark, Aby!" she'll say, and the child, eager to do grown-up work, to be her partner, to build the beautiful, dangerous fire against the fall of night, cries, "I'll get the wood!" and is off like an erratic, fuzzy-feathered arrow. He searches, stoops, and gathers, rushes back dropping bits of driftwood, dumps his tiny load, and is off again. She gathers methodically. There are plenty of useful pieces of driftwood near the big, half-buried, half-burned log she has chosen as backlog and windbreak. Soon she has her woodpile, and begins to lean sticks up against the charred monster, over the hollow where she has arranged a tight-crumpled sheet of news-paper and bits of fine kindling. It won't be a big blaze. Huge, flaring bonfires that roar and volley out sparks are frightening to Aby, and to her too. It will be a small, bright, clear fire in this vast, clear, bright evening.

Aby will come up breathless with a "very big log"—a branch three feet long at least, and so heavy he has to drag it. She will praise the wood and the woodsman. Kneeling,

American Short Fiction, Volume 2, Number 7, Fall 1992
© *1992 Ursula K. Le Guin*

putting her bare arm round his thin shoulders, she'll say, "Aby, love, look," and they'll look into the west.

"That's where the sun was," Aby will say, pointing to the center source of the immense, pale-pink rays of light that fan out, barely visible, in the far air suffused with gold above the sea.

"And that's the shadow of the earth." She will look up at the blue dimness that has risen from the mountains in the east to the top of the sky just over them.

"Yeah!" says Aby, delighted with it all, and wriggles free. "Look, there's a even *bigger* log!" And he's off.

"When you come back we'll light the fire," she calls, feeling for the matches in her pocket. She sits down on the warm sand to watch the great rosy shafts of light shorten down and down into the darkening horizon. The breakers are quiet and regular, six or seven lines of them. Their huge noise all up and down the beach masks all lesser sounds except the rare cries of gulls flying late. No one else has a fire on the beach tonight, no one is walking down by the waterline.

When she first hears the drumming, she thinks it is a helicopter, a Coast Guard patrol, and looks south for the black dot in the air; but her eye catches the movement nearer, down by the breakers, as she hears the drum-drum-drum of hooves on hard sand. The horse is at full gallop, the rider leans lightly forward, riding bareback— Beautiful! the double silhouette black against shining sand, the wild rhythm, the courage to ride at a gallop bareback! On to the north they go, fading into the dusk and the faint mist that hovers over the meeting of the water and the land. Oh, what a sight! She wishes he would come back, the centaur galloping between sea and sand, between daylight and the dark. And soon from the north comes the drum-drum-drum more felt than heard, and horse and rider take shape in the low mist, cantering now, lightly, easily. They slow and turn a little, and dropping into a walk come up across the sand to her. They halt. The horse raises his head and shakes it. He wears only a rope bridle with a single rein. "I saw you lighting the fire," the rider says.

She stands up, she puts her hand out to the horse, a dark bay with a blaze that gleams white in the twilight. She strokes the soft nose and reaches up to scratch under the sweaty forelock and around the roots of the big, delicate, flicking ears. The rider smiles. He vaults down from the horse's back. Like a cowboy, he simply drops the rein, and the horse nickers once and stands quiet. Oh, she knows this cowboy, this centaur, this bareback rider. "Where have you been riding?" she asks, and he answers, "Along the seacoast of Bohemia," smiling.

The fire has just caught. She adds a stout, barky branch which flares up at once. They sit down, one on each side, each seeing the other's face across the quivering flames, which seem to darken the twilight and draw it in around them.

"No," she says, "not Bohemia. Hungary. You've been riding with the Magyars again."

"All across the steppes," he says in his laughing voice, soft and resonant. "With the warrior hordes. Coming to loot the West."

"And the women follow along behind with the children and the colts and the tents and the beds. . . ."

"They light the fires. And the men turn around and come back to the fires."

"And my man comes around to my side of the fire," she says, and he does: a quiet movement, a warmth along her side, a warm arm round her shoulders. She turns to him and comes into his arms. The dark head bends to her: a long kiss, longer, deeper. Firelight webs rainbows in her lashes. The sand is warm and soft, a dark bed, an endless bed, its rumpled sheets the breakers glimmering.

Sleepy, she looks straight up into the shadow of the world and sees Vega, the star always at the top of the summer night. The linchpin, the keystone, the white thumbtack that holds the whole sky up. Oh, hello, she murmurs to the star. The spangle of the Milky Way is not yet visible, only the four stars of the Swan burning faint in the turquoise-cobalt sky.

The sand is still warm from the long day's sunlight, but not really soft. After a while you always remember, when you lie on it, that sand is stone. She sits up and gazes into the fire, then builds it up, adding a couple of long branches that can be shoved in farther as they burn, keeping it steady. Twigs flare up bright for a moment. Looking down the beach, now nearly dark, a faint blur of mist still hovering over the breakers, she imagines how the fire must look from down there at the waterline: a warm star, flickering, earthy. She wants to see it. She gets up, stretches, and walks slowly down to the wet sand. She does not look back till her bare feet feel the cold of the water. Then she turns and gazes at the fire up under the dunes.

It is very small, a little trembling brightness in the vast blur of dark blue-gray that has taken away the mountains. There is no other brightness but the stars. She shivers and runs, runs straight back up the sand, back to her fire, back to its warmth where two women sit in silence, one on each side, gazing into the flames. Their tanned, lined faces are lit ruddy and deeply shadowed. She sits down between them, a little breathless, her back to the sea.

"How's the water?" one of them asks, and she says only, "Brrr!"

"When was it we went to the beach at Santa Cruz?" the older woman asks the younger, who answers, "Right after the war. Wasn't it? I remember complaining about picnics with no hard-boiled eggs."

"Spam. Terrible stuff. Salted grease, think of it! She was just a baby. Three, maybe?"

"More like five?"

Their voices have always been quiet, never final. There is always a leaving open, a possibility of question.

"I remember we had a fire on the beach, against a drift-log, like this. We sat so late. Yes, it was then, because I remember thinking, no war out there, and it was hard to believe, after so long, that it was just the sea out there again. We were talking. She'd been asleep for ages. Curled up on the blanket. All of a sudden, out of nowhere, she said, 'Mama, will it go on forever?' Do you remember that? I never knew if she was awake or dreaming."

"We'd been trying to remember names of constellations. I remember. She must have been half awake; she was looking at the fire. 'Will it go on forever?' And you said yes. 'Yes, it will.' And she settled down again, perfectly satisfied."

"Did I? Did I really? I'd forgotten. . . ." They laughed quietly, little soft, grunting laughs. She looked from one face to the other: a good deal alike, though one was webbed and cragged and the other still full, with a soft underlip. The deepset eyes glinted in the firelight.

"Oh," she said, "oh but it didn't—it doesn't— Does it?"

They looked at her, four tiny warm fires glinting and trembling in their eyes. Did they laugh? They were smiling. Outside the circle of the firelight a man spoke briefly and a woman answered him. "How about another piece of wood?" one of the men said, and she looked at her fire and decided it was time for the piece she had been saving, the massive trunk end of a large branch, perfectly dry. She laid it with care in the bright center where it would catch fast and burn hot. Sparks flew up into the air that was now quite dark. All the stars hung over the fire, over the sea. The path of the Galaxy whitened the quiet water far out beyond the breakers. Now and then a flash of light broke across the sand: luminous water, tiny sea-beings, sea-fireflies. The mist was gone, the dark was clear. The company of the stars shone brighter than the brief gleams among the breakers.

The fire creaked and crackled, and the damp core of a log hissed and sang. They all sat or lay near the flames as the night grew cooler, her people, some talking softly, others stargazing or sleeping. Aby had long been asleep, curled up on the blanket beside her. She pulled the blanket back over his bare legs. He wriggled and made a protest in his dream. "There," she murmured. "It will. Yes, it will, love." Up in the dunes one of the horses snorted. The sound of the sea was low and long and deep, a huge roar up and down the edge of the land, too large to listen to for long. Sometimes a warmer breath of wind moved seaward, smelling of soil and summer, and a few sparks flew out on it for a moment.

She got up at last, stiff. She slowly covered over the embers with cold sand. When that was done, she climbed the dunes alone in starlight toward the moon, which had not risen yet.   ◆

URSULA K. LE GUIN's novels *The Left Hand of Darkness* and *The Dispossessed* are classics of the science-fiction genre. Her short fiction appears regularly in such magazines as *The New Yorker*. Her story "Texts" appeared in *American Short Fiction* Number 1, Spring 1991. She lives in the Pacific Northwest.

EPOCH

SINCE 1947   FICTION, POETRY, ESSAYS

Published
three times
per year.

Sample
copy
$4.00

One year
subscription
$11.00

Painting (detail) by Richard Estell. Courtesy of Ruth Siegel Gallery, New York

Available from 251 Goldwin Smith Hall, Cornell University, Ithaca, NY 14853

JML

Editor: **Morton P. Levitt**

Founding Editor: **Maurice Beebe**

Covering the literary history of the twentieth century, **JML** is devoted to scholarly analyses of Modernist and Post-Modernist literatures and to the cross-fertilization of the arts. Our coverage now includes world literature.

Special Issues

William Carlos Williams • Nikos Kazantzakis • Film and Literature • William Butler Yeats • Gotham Book Mart • Modernism and Post-Modernism • Samuel Beckett • Franz Kafka • E. E. Cummings • John Fowles • Ezra Pound

Annual Review Issues

Our unique A/R issues review the major books published each year in the field and list as well the articles, dissertations, special numbers, and general information on modern literature published in the United States and throughout the world.

Domestic Subscriptions
$16/Individuals
$20/Institutions

Foreign Subscriptions
$20/Individuals
$25/Institutions

Individual Issues
$5/General $6/Foreign
$ 10/Annual Review $12/Foreign

JOURNAL OF MODERN LITERATURE
921 Anderson Hall
Temple University
Philadelphia, Pennsylvania 19122

TriQuarterly

Fiction • Poetry • Art • Criticism

$18/year
$32/2 years

2020 Ridge Ave.
Evanston, IL 60208

DRAWING BY PETER DE SEVE. *(TQ #56)*

The ANTIOCH REVIEW
50th Anniversary Issue

The Best Words in the Best Order

Over 450 pages

Volume 50, numbers 1 & 2 • Winter/Spring 1992 • $12.95, plus $2.00 postage

Daniel Bell	Elizabeth Fox-Genovese	Sylvia Plath
Jorge Luis Borges	Clifford Geertz	David Riesman
T. Coraghessan Boyle	Allen Ginsberg	Anne Sexton
Raymond Carver	Andrew Greeley	Elaine Showalter
Robert Creeley	Denise Levertov	Mark Strand
William Dickey	Philip Levine	William Trevor
Annie Dillard	Gordon Lish	Richard Wilbur
Ralph Ellison	Cynthia Ozick	Joy Williams

The Antioch Review, P.O. Box 148, Yellow Springs, OH 45387

$\mathcal{A}$MERICAN
$\mathcal{S}$HORT
$\mathcal{F}$ICTION

Laura Furman, *Editor*
University of Texas at Austin

Contents of Next Issue, Number 8, Winter 1992

Rick Bass	*The Valley*
Janet Peery	*Daughter of the Moon*
Robert Spencer Wilson	*Safe at Home*
John Keeble	*The Fishers*
Richard McCann	*Fugitive Light, Old Photos*
Paula Huston	*Mercy*
John Rolfe Gardiner	*Morse Operator*

American Short Fiction, published quarterly in Spring, Summer, Fall, and Winter, is available by subscription. Subscriptions begin with the Spring issue.

Subscription rates: Individuals, $24; Institutions, $36 Outside USA, add $5.50/subscription.
Money order, check or credit card orders accepted.
Prepayment required.

Name _____

Address _____

_____

City _____

State _____ Zip _____

Please charge my subscription to:
_____ VISA _____ MC _____ AM EXPRESS
Account # _____
Exp. date _____
Phone # _____
Signature _____
Total amount enclosed $ _____

Reply to: Journals Department, University of Texas Press, Box 7819, Austin, Texas 78713